# The 47 People You'll Meet in Middle School

## Also by Kristin Mahoney

*Annie's Life in Lists*

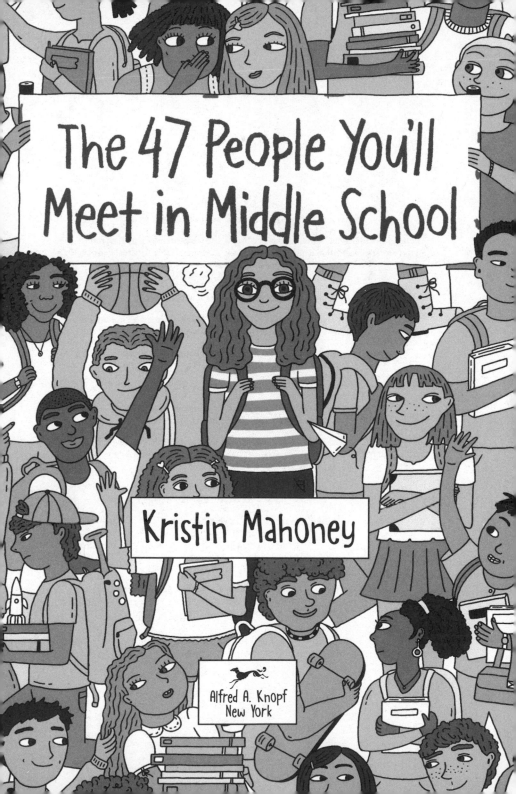

THIS IS A BORZOI BOOK PUBLISHED BY ALFRED A. KNOPF

This is a work of fiction. Names, characters, places, and incidents either are the product of the author's imagination or are used fictitiously. Any resemblance to actual persons, living or dead, events, or locales is entirely coincidental.

Text copyright © 2019 by Kristin Mahoney
Jacket art and interior illustrations copyright © 2019 by Hyesu Lee

All rights reserved. Published in the United States by Alfred A. Knopf, an imprint of Random House Children's Books, a division of Penguin Random House LLC, New York.

Knopf, Borzoi Books, and the colophon are registered trademarks of Penguin Random House LLC.

Visit us on the Web! rhcbooks.com

Educators and librarians, for a variety of teaching tools, visit us at RHTeachersLibrarians.com

Library of Congress Cataloging-in-Publication Data is available upon request.
ISBN 978-1-5247-6513-2 (trade) — ISBN 978-1-5247-6514-9 (lib. bdg.)
ISBN 978-1-5247-6515-6 (ebook)

The text of this book is set in 12-point Sabon LT.
The illustrations were created digitally.

Printed in the United States of America
August 2019
10 9 8 7 6 5 4

First Edition

*For*
*Alice and Lucy,*
*the sisters who teach me so much*

*May you always find your people*

*Let us be grateful to the people who
make us happy; they are the charming
gardeners who make our souls blossom.*
　　　　　　　—Marcel Proust


*I get by with a little help from
my friends.*
　　　　　　　—The Beatles

*Dear Louisa,*

*Today was the last day of school before Thanksgiving break. The end of my first few months of sixth grade. Since school started, you've been asking me what middle school is like. And since then, I've been saying things like "It's fine, whatever." I know this is not a helpful answer. I know you are dying to know what to expect when you start at Meridian Middle School in two years. I know I'm supposed to give you the scoop, show you the ropes, hand you the keys (and a bunch of other clichés Mom and Dad used), because I'm your big sister.*

*The truth is, I'm still figuring it out myself. It's only been a few months, and it's hard to respond to questions when you're still working on the answers. And the fact that <u>this</u> particular school year has started out* *as the weirdest ever . . . well, that hasn't helped.*

*But I will say I've had time to reflect on your question over the past couple of days. (You know how you don't really do anything during the last few days of school before a break? That's still true in middle school.) So while the teachers have been showing movies and tidying up their classrooms and the other kids have been passing notes and falling asleep at their desks or doodling on their sneakers, I've been reflecting. (<u>Reflecting</u> is a big thing middle-school teachers are into. You'll see.)*

*So, what is middle school like, you ask? (And ask, and ask.)*

*There are a few things I can tell you:*

1. *It's nothing like elementary school.*
2. *Lockers are not as exciting as everyone thinks they'll be.*
3. *You might be on your own without some of your closest friends. Take me and Layla, for example. She's been my best friend since we were three, and all through elementary school at Starling.*

But *Starling kids split up for middle school, and just because she lives one street over from us, she has to go to Parkwood Middle School and we have to go to Meridian. So I had to start a new school without my oldest and closest friend.*

4. *You will have no idea where to go. I don't just mean getting lost in the building (although that happens), but you won't know which people to go to, because you won't know who <u>your people</u> are. You may think you will, but you won't. More on that later.*

5. *The time goes by differently. For one thing, you change classes and teachers for each subject, which sounds like it would make the day go faster. But with certain teachers, it actually makes fifty minutes feel like a year. Like, you look at the clock, and then look up at it again about a month later (or so you think), and it has advanced one minute.*

6. *Time passes differently in other ways too. In elementary school, you talk a lot*

*about the seasons: the changing leaves, the snow in winter, the flowers in spring. There's a harvest festival, a Thanksgiving celebration, a winter concert, a spring fair. They have some of that stuff in middle school. But mostly the year passes with people. The people you notice right away. The people you notice much later. The ones who notice you way before you notice them. And vice versa. The people will surprise you. For better and for worse.*

*So the best way to tell you about middle school is to give you a heads-up about the people you'll meet. Sure, some of these might be different for you in a couple of years . . . but this should give you a pretty good idea. Besides, all I can tell you is how it happened for me. So here you go, Lou. These are the people you'll meet in middle school.*

*Love,*

*Augusta*

# 1. The assistant principal

I wish I could tell you that the first person I saw on the first day of school was someone I knew. It was not.

I made Dad drop me off two blocks from school that morning. This was partly because I wasn't sure what the routine was in middle school, and I didn't want to be the only kid whose parent took them right to the front door. But this was *mostly* because Dad's car was in the shop again and—as you may recall from the first day of school, Lou—he had borrowed the radio-station van to drive for a few days. Some people's parents have a clean, fancy company car to drive for work; lucky us that our dad gets a bright green van that actually has WOLD: YOUR FA-VORITE OLDIES painted on the side in orange letters. For first-day-of-school arrival? No thank you.

As I rounded the corner by Meridian Middle, I saw

a crowd of kids who were all complete strangers. They also all looked way older than me. And they seemed like they all knew each other. I knew that more than half the kids at Meridian Middle were coming from a different elementary school than ours, but it still seemed like I should know *someone*. I started wondering if I was in the right place.

Turns out, I was not. And apparently I had *I am in sixth grade—please help me* written on my forehead, because a teacher holding a clipboard actually pointed at me and yelled across the heads of the other kids, "You! Glasses! Blue backpack! Sixth grade?"

You wouldn't think that "glasses" and "blue backpack" would be sufficient identifiers. I mean, other kids had glasses and blue backpacks. But I guess this teacher's pointing was laser-sharp, because about a hundred kids turned and looked right at me after he yelled.

"Um, yes?" I answered, almost in a whisper (and still wondering where the heck everyone I knew was).

"What was that?"

"Yes. Sixth," I said, slightly louder.

"Back door!" the teacher yelled. "Didn't your parents get the email?"

By this point the teacher was making his way over, clapping students on the back, saying hello, and telling some of them to spit out their gum. He was wearing a golf shirt with the school logo on it. The shirt strained over his belly and was tucked snugly into his khaki pants. I wondered how he got his shirt to stay tucked so tight, especially with a big belly. Did he buy extra-long shirts?

"Did your parents get the email?" he asked again.

"I'm not sure?" I said. Since the weekend before school started had been one of our weekends at Dad's apartment, it was possible I wasn't operating with complete information. (You know he's not so great about reading emails thoroughly.) I began to wonder what else he'd missed.

"Well," the teacher explained, "this is the eighth-grade entrance. Sixth graders go to the back."

"Oh, okay." That seemed pretty inhospitable to me, making the new kids go to the back door. But I wasn't going to argue. I turned and started walking down the path that wound around to the back of the building.

"Heeey, Little Gus!" I heard someone call. I knew it had to be a kid from our neighborhood, since he was calling me Gus and not Augusta. I turned and, sure enough, there was Rob Vinson, talking to some other eighth-grade boys. Even though Rob is kind of dopey, he's usually an okay kid. He's always been Mom and

Dad's first choice to walk Iris when we're gone on a day trip somewhere, and he was never jerky to us like some of the other older neighborhood boys were. So hearing his familiar voice on the first day of school was simultaneously comforting and embarrassing. (*Why* did he have to call me Little Gus in front of everyone else? Ugh.)

"It's my neighbor!" Rob announced, not that the boys he was with seemed to care.

"What are you doing on this side of the building, Little Gus?" he asked.

"I got the entrance wrong. That teacher told me to go around back," I said, pointing to the man with the super-tight tuck-in.

"That's not a teacher, Gus," Rob said. "That's an assistant principal. Mr. Wyatt. You don't want to tangle with him."

"I didn't tangle with him," I said. "He just told me I had the wrong door."

"Okay, well, watch yourself with that one. If he told you to go to the back door, you'd better go fast. Why are you still standing here?"

"Because you're still talking to me!"

"Nah, you better go, Little Gus!" Rob shooed me away like I was a pesky dog, never mind that he had been the one detaining me.

I rolled my eyes and went around to the back of the building. And that's where I saw all the kids I knew. All the kids whose parents had read the email properly.

That night I got in a fight with Mom because I told her she needed to make sure Dad read his emails all the way through. And I may have said something like "If you guys still lived together, we wouldn't have these problems." And then Mom felt like dirt, and so did I.

I don't know if you remember that fight, Lou, or if you even heard it. You were standing at the kitchen sink making one of your "potions." (This one contained olive oil, flower petals, and dish soap.) It seemed like you were in your own world. Until you announced that the potion was going to be a special doggy-fur conditioner for Iris, and Mom took one look at it and said there was no way you were going to rub olive oil on the dog.

That's when you snapped back into our world and asked what we were talking about, and I just said, "School." That was the first time you asked me to tell you what middle school was like. That was the first time I said, "It's fine, whatever," and went upstairs to my room.

Anyway, now you know a little. Sixth graders go to the back door. And don't tangle with Mr. Wyatt. He was the first person I met in middle school. And unfortunately, I would meet him again.

# 2. The friend you don't recognize because she turned into a whole new person over the summer

I figured that as I rounded the corner to the back of the building, everything would fall into place. I'd be surrounded by people I knew, and middle school would start feeling the way it was supposed to. And for a second, it did. I spotted Jason Cordrey, Mekhai Curry, and a few other boys I'd known since kindergarten. They looked the same, and they were doing just what they always did last year: trying to spin each other around by their backpack straps.

The next person I recognized was Addison Aldrich, standing near a picnic bench with the same pose she'd had every day as she held court during recess in fifth grade: backpack loosely hanging off one shoulder, right leg ramrod straight, and left foot poised on tiptoe, as though the ballet flats she owns in every color were actual toe shoes. Addison and I had never really hit it off. We tried being friends for about five minutes in second grade, but then she dared me to smear peanut butter on Jason Cordrey's pencil. Jason has a bad peanut allergy. I wouldn't do it. Addison called me a chicken, flipped her hair at me, and walked away. Yeah. She was a hair flipper already in second grade. Enough said.

Anyway, on the first day of school Addison was talking to a girl who looked familiar. I figured the girl must be in seventh grade, or even eighth, because she was tall, with huge hoop earrings, and maybe even had a little bit of makeup on? No one I knew in my grade wore makeup yet, not even the girls in Addison's crowd.

I heard someone yell, "Hey, Marcy!" and I looked around. The only Marcy I knew was Marcy Shea. I never told you this, but even though Marcy and I had been friends since first grade, she was kind of bugging me last year. Layla was in a different fifth-grade class, and we weren't allowed to sit with other classes in the cafeteria. So Marcy always had to sit beside me at lunch, put her sleeping bag beside mine at slumber parties, and ask if I would ride on the bus with her on field trips (like a month before the trips even happened, just to make sure there was no chance I'd sit with anyone else). I don't know why it bugged me so much; I'd never minded hanging out with her before. It just felt like at the same time Marcy needed to be together constantly, I started needing to be in my own space more. Not just around Marcy, but with other people too. Mom. Dad. You. (Sorry.)

It was like I didn't just need physical space; I also needed space in my head. For all the things I was starting to wonder about more, like what other people thought of me, and whether my jeans were too short or my laugh was too loud or my water bottle was a stupid color.

I felt like I needed space to think about other things too, specifically all the extra thoughts I was having after Mom and Dad told us they were splitting up. I mean, some of the things they brought up in that conversation were things that never even would have occurred to me, but now they were all I could think about. Like when Mom said, "We want you to know this isn't your fault." Well, yeah. Did you ever for a second think that the divorce was our fault, Lou? I didn't. What could we have done to make our parents get divorced? Sheesh. And when Dad said, "We will find a way to make this work, and you will not have to go to court to choose between us." Ummmm, okay. I never even knew that was a thing that could really happen. But now I was thinking, *Wait . . . could that really happen?* And the way Mom laughed nervously and said "Of course not!" after Dad brought it up made me wonder even more.

I don't know about you, but when I am thinking thoughts like *Am I going to have to choose between my parents in court?* or even *Why am I the only one in this class with an orange water bottle?*, it makes me feel— I don't know—prickly. And if someone grabs my arm and says "Sit beside me on the bus!" while I'm quietly wondering if I'm to blame for my parents' divorce, well . . . sometimes it's all I can do not to jerk my arm away and yell, "Sit by yourself!"

But I never did that. As much as Marcy annoyed me, I was never very good at saying no to her (even in a less dramatic way), so we wound up beside each other at a lot of lunches and slumber parties, and on a lot of field-trip buses. Her family was going to be away in Nova Scotia for most of the summer, and I was relieved to be getting a break from her.

On the last day of fifth grade, Marcy had told me we had to "strategize" for the first day of middle school. She said she'd call me when she got back from her vacation so we could coordinate our outfits, transportation, and arrival time for the first day. I was a little surprised when I never heard from her, but mostly I felt like I'd dodged a clingy bullet. For all I knew, she'd moved to Canada for good.

So on the first day of school, when a kid hollered "Marcy," the last person I expected to respond was the tall, lipstick-wearing, hoop-earringed girl talking to Addison. But sure enough, it was her. I could see it now. Under the makeup and between the hoop earrings, her face was a longer, narrower version of the Marcy who'd plunked her lunch box down beside mine every day in the cafeteria last year.

"Hey, girl!" Marcy yelled to the kid who'd called her name, raising skyward an arm full of bangle bracelets that were only a little bigger than her giant hoop earrings.

She noticed me standing there as her arm came back down and said, "Oh—hey, Augusta," in a voice that was suddenly way less enthusiastic.

Before I could even say hi back, Addison grabbed Marcy's arm and inspected one of the bangle bracelets. "Ooh!" she squealed. "Is this the one you got the day we went whale-watching?"

"You guys went whale-watching together?" I asked.

"Yes!" Addison squealed again. "This year Marcy's family summered in the same spot where my family always summers. We went on a whale-and-dolphin watch together."

"You *summered* there, huh?" Louie, I know you (and Mom, and Dad) always hate my sarcastic tone, but this was ridiculous. Who uses "summer" as a verb? And twice in the same sentence?

"Yes. We *spent the summer* there. *Summered,*" Marcy explained, like I was an idiot. "My parents say we can go back every year now."

"We summered here in Meridian," a voice behind me said. "My parents say we'll do that every year too." I turned and saw Nick Zambrano spinning a Frisbee on his index finger. Marcy rolled her eyes and turned back around.

"Hey, Gus," Nick said. "Thought I was gonna be late this morning. My parents didn't read the email and I went to the front door."

I said hi back to Nick, but I was too distracted to really pay attention to him. With her new long legs and made-up face and "summering" in Nova Scotia, Marcy looked like a different kind of creature from the rest of us. *Do I seem any different from last year?* I wondered. This was something I couldn't really get a handle on: how I came off to other people. (That was another thing I was sometimes wondering about when I felt like

I needed space: What kind of person did I seem like?) I tried quickly glancing down at myself to see if I looked that different from last year. I had new sneakers. My hair was a little longer. That was about it. Nothing like the new-and-improved Marcy.

I know what you're thinking, Louie: *That couldn't happen to any of my friends!* Trust me. It will. In fact, from your crew of kids, my money's on Isabella. Look how much she's changed already since kindergarten, when she used to cry at drop-off every morning. Now she plays travel lacrosse, and she spent the summer at cheerleading camp. Mark my words: On the first day of sixth grade, you may not know who she is.

# 3. Your homeroom teacher

Here's what you should know about homeroom: There's not much homey about it. Since it's the first place you go in the morning, I think I imagined it was going to be where we had morning meetings, the way you do in elementary school. Everyone would gather on the rug or circle their chairs and talk about current events, plans we had for the weekend, or anything at all that was on our minds. And last year, since my fifth-grade teacher was Mr. Singer and he filled his classroom with a cozy sofa and a soft rug and string lights across the tops of the windows and everyone thought he was pretty much the greatest teacher ever . . . well, our class really did feel like home sometimes. (Which was especially good last year when life in our actual home started getting pretty weird.)

But in sixth grade . . . no. In middle school, homeroom is all business. Or at least it is for me, maybe because my homeroom teacher is also the actual business teacher, Mr. Smeed. As the year has gone on, we've learned that Mr. Smeed has a small collection of light brown, light green, and light yellow short-sleeved button-down shirts that he wears with ties in corresponding shades. Mr. Smeed also seems to be really worried about having bad breath. This we know because he keeps a little container of breath spray in his shirt pocket. The breath spray is called Binaca, and he sprays it into his mouth at least three times during every homeroom session.

On the first day of school, Mr. Smeed assigned us all office-type jobs like "accountant" (collects money for school events), "parliamentarian" (makes sure Mr. Smeed's not forgetting anything he's supposed to do), "recording secretary" (writes down any questions Mr. Smeed needs to research the answers to), and "file clerk." I got file clerk. (I would soon find out that that was a big job the first week of school, because we all had to bring back a bunch of signed forms from our parents, and I had to file them in just the right way in Mr. Smeed's color-coded folders. If anything was garbage, he'd point to the recycling bin and say "put that one in file thirteen" and chuckle, like calling the trash can file thirteen was the funniest joke ever.)

Nick Zambrano was parliamentarian. "I don't know what that means," he said when Mr. Smeed gave him the assignment.

"It means you keep us on schedule and in order!" Mr. Smeed explained (before spraying Binaca into his mouth). "And don't assume I'm always going to do things the right way; I've been known to make mistakes on purpose just to make sure my parliamentarian is paying attention!"

"Okaaaay," Nick said. He turned to me and whispered, "What's up with this guy?"

I shrugged. "I think he thinks this is his business."

"So we're his employees?"

"Something like that."

"Mr. Zambrano and Ms. Reynolds!" Suddenly Mr. Smeed was standing between our desks, consulting a desk chart on his clipboard to make sure he had our names right. "Is there a matter of business between the parliamentarian and the file clerk that I should be aware of?"

"No," Nick said.

"No, what?" Mr. Smeed asked.

"No . . . there isn't?" Nick answered.

Oh boy. "No, Mr. Smeed," I said. "We're fine."

"Well, next time you two have to have a conversation, do it on your own time. This is my time," Mr. Smeed said, then took another hit of Binaca.

I guess he expected some kind of response from us because when we didn't say anything, he said, "Is that understood?" in an even louder voice than he'd used before.

"Yes," we both answered. Then, when he kept staring at us, we added, "Mr. Smeed."

The bell rang for us to go to first period, so I scooped up all the papers Mr. Smeed had handed out and stuffed them in my backpack.

"That's not very organized procedure for a file clerk, Ms. Reynolds," Mr. Smeed said, watching me. "I will expect much more careful handling of the files in this classroom." *(Spray spray.)*

I nodded at him, but he seemed to expect more. Did he want me to reorganize the papers right then and there? I had to get to my first-period class.

"Okay," I said. "I will work on, um, organizing my procedures. Mr. Smeed." I guess that wasn't exactly the response he wanted either, because he just squinted at me as I hoisted my backpack onto my shoulder. And I think Mr. Smeed heard the same thing I did: Nick stifling a laugh as we headed out the door to first period.

# 4. The disappointing turtle

Remember when we were little and Mom and Dad used to take us to feed the ducks at the pond in Orchard Park and we always looked for turtles? After all the bread scraps were gone, we'd go to the end of the pond that was thick with lily pads and stare and stare until we spotted a turtle. It wasn't easy because of the way they blended in with the lily pads. But eventually, we'd make out little dark green turtle shells and heads bobbing up through the light green of the lily-pad stew.

Do you remember that whoever spotted a turtle first would yell "Turtle Top"? (I'm not sure why we said that . . . I guess it was because we could only see the top of the turtle?) Anyway, I remember it was always a big competition, seeing who could yell "Turtle Top" first. And Iris would bark and bark if she saw the turtle too.

And then whoever didn't spot the turtle first would get mad at the person who did, then we'd get in a big fight about who had really seen it first, and then Mom and Dad would get exasperated and suggest that we go for ice cream just to distract us and make us stop fighting. And it always worked. That was a really long time ago, huh? I think the last couple of times all four of us went, Mom and Dad were on their phones the whole time. And then, eventually, they started taking us separately. Maybe we stopped playing Turtle Top because we were getting older, or maybe it's because it wasn't nearly as much fun without all four of us there.

Anyway, the first day of middle school reminded me of trying to spot turtles in the pond. Because I was walking through this big crowd of kids I didn't recognize, and their faces all blended together the way the lily pads did. But then, once in a while, a familiar face would bob up out of the crowd, and I had to bite my tongue to keep from shouting "Turtle Top!" I wanted to, though. I also wished that you were there with me to fight about who'd seen the turtle first, and that Mom and Dad were about to take us for ice cream.

Well, the "turtle" I saw in the hall after homeroom that day was Natalie Daniels, as I was walking to my first-period class, science. She wasn't exactly first on the list of turtles I would have wanted to see, considering how she'd spent most of fifth grade doodling *Dance Girls Rule!* on all her notebooks, but still, she was a familiar face.

"Hey, Natalie!" I said with way more excitement than I usually had for her. "Where's your first class?"

"It's science. So I think it's in the science wing. I don't know. Are all science classes in the science wing? Where is the science wing? My first class is science."

"Riiight . . . you said that," I reminded her. She seemed a little manic. "I'm going to science too. Who's your teacher?"

She looked at her schedule. "Warren. It says Warren. Do you think that's a man or a woman? Who's yours?"

"Mine is McCabe," I answered, starting to feel a little relieved that we'd be in different classes.

"Oh no," Natalie said, as though I'd just told her she'd never dance again. "What's your room number?"

I checked my schedule again. "128."

"Okay, I'm 126," she said. "126! They must be near each other. We can walk together! Make sure you talk to me the whole time, okay? I don't want people to think we don't have anything to talk about."

So for the next five minutes I half listened as Natalie babbled nervously about finding her classes, decorating her locker, and, of course, going to dance-team auditions. When we got to the science wing and found our classes, I saw a couple of kids give us weird looks after she gave my hand a squeeze and said "Okay! Good luck in science!" a little too loudly.

I guess the moral of this story is, be wary of familiar faces on the first day of middle school. If you grab on to a tiny turtle to stay afloat, you'll probably just wind up sinking to the bottom.

Natalie would be okay, by the way. I saw her run on tiptoe to one of her dance friends after she walked into Mr. Warren's classroom.

As for me, I was facing a brand-new sea of lily pads in room 128.

# 5. The scary teacher

I know you don't think you need me to tell you about scary teachers, Lou. I know you think Ms. Chesser, who you had in second grade, was scary because she only let kids go to the bathroom once a day. (I know this because you'd come home every day and tell Mom and Dad all the bathroom details we didn't need to know. Like whether you went number one or number two, and how you had to hold it in forever and ever because of mean Ms. Chesser, and once you even wet your pants a little. You've always told Mom and Dad *way* more than I have about things like that. Bathroom information. Body-ailment information. Crush information. Friend-drama information. Too much information.)

Anyway, I also know you'll hear stories about scary middle-school teachers from other kids before you get to Meridian. Those stories spread like crazy; I know because I'd heard them too. The gym teacher who was in the Mafia. The history teacher who'd been arrested during a botched toy-store robbery. The science teacher who slams a wooden bat onto the desks of kids who aren't paying attention.

Well, I can tell you that at least one of these is true. I don't know much about any Meridian teachers with lives in organized (or disorganized) crime, but I can tell you that Mr. McCabe patrols the aisles of his classroom with a bat perched on his shoulder, kind of like a cartoon caveman with a club. And he *does* bring the bat down when kids least expect it. Oh, and the bat has a name. It's Lorenzo.

He was holding it on the first day of school as he stood in the doorway of his classroom. He and the bat had matching name tags (HELLO, MY NAME IS MR. MCCABE and HELLO, MY NAME IS LORENZO). He told each of us to find our own name tag on a table by the front door. I started looking for AUGUSTA until I realized the name tags just had last names on them, so finally I found my REYNOLDS name tag and sat down in the fourth row of desks.

I watched as a stream of kids I didn't know (I guess they'd gone to Minter Elementary) walked in and looked for their name tags. Eventually a few kids from Starling walked in, but no one that interesting: Sharla Yingst, David Martin, and—again—Nick Zambrano, who sat across from me and immediately asked to borrow a pencil.

Mr. McCabe used to be a Marine. I think that's why he calls us all by our last names. He also says things like "If a good Marine has only ten minutes to rest, he can fall asleep in one minute and get nine good minutes of shut-eye." The first time he told us that, Nick of course yelled, "How about we try that now!" which earned his desk a visit from Lorenzo.

Mr. McCabe has traveled all over the world, and as the year has gone on, we've learned that if we play our cards right, we can distract him and get him to tell us all about eating roast guinea pig in Peru or riding an elephant in Kenya. Not only are the stories fascinating, but the more time he spends telling them, the less time we have to discuss amoebas or the periodic table of elements.

We were in Mr. McCabe's class the day in September when Principal Olin made an announcement over the intercom asking for volunteers for the social committee, whose first job would be to plan the November dance. (She said it was going to be a Sadie Hawkins dance, which meant that girls were supposed to invite boys as dates or invite the boys to dance once we got there. More on that later, but in a nutshell: no thank you.)

Mr. McCabe had thoughts about the Sadie Hawkins dance. Not about the girls-inviting-boys aspect, but about the dancing.

"I don't know why they even call it dancing anymore," he said with a sigh. "In my day, we danced. What you kids do is shadowboxing." (I had to google "shadowboxing" when I got home. It means "practice fighting with an invisible opponent." I'm not sure I got Mr. McCabe's point, but it was an interesting metaphor for a middle-school dance.)

I'll tell you who wasn't shadowboxing, though. Three girls from Minter who were all in Mr. McCabe's first-period science class too. They seemed to be having the time of their lives.

# 6. The Huggers

Okay, so technically this is three people, not one person. But they function as a unit, so I'm counting them as one. As I sat and watched kids file into Mr. McCabe's room that first day, I noticed that some (like me) walked in alone and quickly found a name tag and a seat. Others walked in with one friend, or said a quiet "hey" to someone they recognized.

And then there were the Huggers.

Three girls from Minter were among the last to arrive to science, and when they saw each other in line at the name-tag table, they squealed, *actually yelled "HUG!"* and then hugged each other.

Then, get this: they did it again at the end of class when they got out of their seats. Later I'd notice them doing it in the lunchroom, at the end of the school day, and in the morning too.

Their names are Hannah, Una, and Gabby. I learned this on the first day of school when Mr. McCabe, tapping Lorenzo on his desk in an agitated rhythm, asked, "When was the last time you ladies saw each other?" as they hugged goodbye.

"We had a sleepover last night!" one of the Huggers said.

"Hmm," Mr. McCabe snorted. "I thought perhaps one of you had just returned from war."

Another Hugger laughed. "No! We've just been best friends forever and our initials are *H-U-G*, so we always have to hug when we say hello or goodbye!" To clarify, she pointed to herself and said, "Hannah," then went down the line and introduced Una and Gabby.

Mr. McCabe looked at them blankly for a second, then said, "Well. The only one who goes by a first name in my classroom is Lorenzo." And he tapped Lorenzo's head on his desk once more, a little louder this time.

If that bothered the Huggers, they didn't show it. They laughed and squeezed through the doorway arm in arm, hugging once more before going their separate ways for second period.

I had several thoughts about the Huggers right off

the bat (no pun intended, Lorenzo). First: They'd had a sleepover together *the night before the first day of school*? What parents would allow that? Maybe their families were super close and *summered* together and ate dinner with each other all the time and they were some of those girls who said "we're more like sisters." As if sisters would actually squeal and hug each other every five minutes.

Second thought: the hugging. Really? Lately I feel like I'm irritated any time another human even touches my arm or pats me on the back. I guess that goes along with the business of needing extra space to think my thoughts, and shrugging off people like Marcy. (Maybe you've noticed too, Louie. Like the last time you tried to braid my hair, and I yelled at you to leave me alone, and you went to your room and slammed the door, and Mom gave us each a talk. My talk was about overreactions and yours was about respecting my personal space.) Anyway, I can't imagine feeling so comfortable with another person (let alone two other people) that every time we saw each other, we'd hug in public. Shudder.

So that was science class. A semi-scary teacher, a baseball bat, and three Huggers. And no one I knew except Nick. I would know more people in the next class. Including one who I'd wish didn't know me at all.

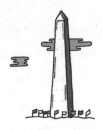

# 7. The teacher who thinks she knows you well

Second period. Social studies. Ms. Tedesco. Do you remember Ms. Tedesco? Probably not, but I guarantee she remembers you. She and Mom took a yoga class together about a hundred years ago, and even though they never hung out or anything, Ms. Tedesco still friended Mom on Facebook and now she thinks she knows everything about us.

For example, on the first day of school Ms. Tedesco went through the roll call and asked each of us what we did over the summer. (I'd hoped we would have outgrown that first-day-of-school ritual by middle school. But no.) When she came to me, she said, "I know what *you* did, Augusta! Art camp! And you and your sister made a giant sandcastle when you were at the beach with your grandparents! Your mom posted some fun pics!"

Suddenly every pair of eyes in the room was on me, no doubt wondering what "fun pics" of my summer Ms. Tedesco had seen that they hadn't.

She laughed. "I'm sorry; I shouldn't have hijacked your turn! Is there anything you want to add?"

Considering she'd already said way more about my summer than I'd planned to, I declined. "No, that's it," I answered, slinking down in my seat and waiting for her to move on to the next kid.

"Okay, well, it looked like a lovely summer! Lucky girl!" she replied, as though I'd gone to Hawaii or Europe and not art camp and Longwood Beach.

"Oh, and before I forget," she added, "did your mom ever find an exterminator? She was looking for someone when you had ants in your bathroom."

"I think it's fine now," I answered over the sound of muffled snickering in the classroom. I prayed Ms. Tedesco would move on. What else had Mom posted about that Ms. Tedesco would mention? Plumbing problems? Kid-underwear recommendations?

Ms. Tedesco's Facebook revelations continued at least once or twice a week, especially when we started studying United States politics. Mom had posted pictures of our trip to Washington, DC, last spring, and Ms. Tedesco acted like that made me some big government expert. Any time she introduced a new point, she'd look at me and say, "Augusta, did you learn anything about this during your trip to Washington?" or "Augusta can probably tell us all about this from her trip to Washington." Nothing makes other kids think you're a weirdo like a teacher treating you like you're her assistant.

But the worst was when she brought up the Smithsonian Museum of American History. As always, she looked at me to ask if we'd gone there, but this time she phrased the question differently. "Did your parents take you to that museum, Augusta?" And without thinking, I answered, "My mom did—yeah."

Then it was like a little light bulb went off for Ms. Tedesco and she murmured, "Oh yes, only your mom. That's right. Forgive me for forgetting." Then her mouth did a downward turn, and I could have sworn I saw her mouth the word "divorce" as she made a little note on her clipboard. With the same expression someone might use while contemplating "cockroaches" or "nuclear war."

Yipes. What do you think she wrote on her clipboard, Lou? A big *D* beside my name? Was she flagging me as though I were now some kind of high-risk case? I leaned over my desk so my hair would hide my face and started tracing an old star doodle with so much pressure that my pen almost poked through the cover of my social-studies notebook.

Ms. Tedesco moved on that day to describing the treasures of the Smithsonian, but I stayed stuck on her weird reaction for a while. Did Mom's happy pictures of our DC trip seem like a lie to Ms. Tedesco once she remembered that only one parent took us?

Not that I really care what Ms. Tedesco thinks. There are other distractions in social studies anyway.

# 8. The kid with questionable hygiene

So far, Lou, it seems like you haven't gotten many of Mom's talks about "changing bodies needing extra care." Probably because your body still hasn't changed all that much. But if you've ever listened to her talk to me, you'll know extra care for changing bodies is a big thing for her. Which is why she makes me shower more than you. And why she bought me deodorant. And a razor.

At first I was annoyed by all the forced showering. But last year during a lockdown drill, I started to see Mom's point. You know how at Starling, when you do a lockdown drill, the whole class has to huddle inside the coat closet? It's no big deal when you're in third grade and your bodies aren't that big yet. It's not even that big of a deal in fifth grade, as long as the weather isn't warm. But our last lockdown drill of the year happened in June, on a day with a high of 92 degrees. So it was easily 100 degrees in the coat closet, maybe even higher once we were all packed in there. I noticed that even Mr. Singer, who was almost always in a peppy mood, rolled his eyes when the lockdown announcement was made that day.

"This is crazy," Marcy said. "Why would they have a lockdown drill on a day that's this hot?"

Natalie Daniels was there beside us. "Maybe it's not a drill," she said. Then of course we were all quiet for a minute while we thought about that. And during that quiet minute, the smells of sweat, fear, and changing bodies that hadn't had enough extra care mingled to create a toxic cloud in the thick air of the coatroom.

By the time the principal's voice came over the loud-speaker to announce the end of the lockdown drill (so it was a drill after all), we were nearly suffocating.

"Wow, the smell in there was something fierce, huh?" Nick said as we walked back to our seats. Marcy and Natalie didn't say anything, and I wondered if they were worried that they were the smelly ones. (I didn't say anything either, for the same reason.)

Anyway, that was the day I started taking showers without being told to. I think most of my fifth-grade class did.

But Gabe Garrett, who I recognized from homeroom and who also sits in front of me in social studies this year, was not in my fifth-grade class. He went to Minter. And either his parents have never talked to him about extra care for changing bodies or he fought the shower battle harder than I did—and won.

So, yeah. Gabe Garrett is smelly. And he has dandruff. Lots of it. And when I try to hide behind him so Ms. Tedesco will stop asking me personal questions, all I can see is a world of dandruff, and I can only look at it for so long before I have to shift positions and risk Ms. Tedesco calling me out again. It's a vicious cycle.

# 9. The kid with the locker above yours

Lou. Maybe you will be lucky. I mean, you usually have been so far. Of the two of us, you're the only one who can turn a cartwheel. And you're way better at braiding hair (when someone lets you). And we both know you're Grandma Nancy's favorite, which is why she gives you jewelry for Christmas and she still gives me twenty-five-piece puzzles.

So maybe you will also be lucky enough to get a top locker in sixth grade. Some sixth graders do, depending on how many kids are in each grade that year.

If you ask me, they should base it on height. For example, a girl who's five foot three inches tall (like me) should not get a bottom locker below a boy who's four foot nine inches tall. Like, for example, Davis Davis. Even if she is in sixth grade and he's in seventh.

What's that you say, Lou? You think you must have read that wrong, because you can't believe anyone would actually be named Davis Davis? Well, believe it. That is his real name. The rumor is that his dad wanted to name him that so that he would be more comfortable when he joined the army someday and his sergeant called him by his last name.

The funny thing is, I think Davis Davis might actually make a decent soldier one day, because his locker is incredibly neat and organized, and he opens it with military speed and precision. At the beginning of the school year, I would still be trying to figure out which books I needed in the amount of time it took for Davis Davis to unlock his lock, open his locker, return the books from his morning classes, take out his books for the afternoon, close his locker, and lock the lock. This was all before I even started turning the dial on my lock, a process that took ages.

At middle-school orientation, the principal will tell you to spend the summer before sixth grade practicing using combination locks. You should listen to her. I didn't.

I guess we could have opened our locks at the same time. But with Davis Davis being the height he is and me being the height I am, it made for an awkward configuration. I'm not just going to barrel over to my bottom locker while he's standing at his top locker. You know how I need my personal space. Luckily, it seems that Davis Davis is the same way. So as I tried to get my lock open, on the first day of school, he stood off to the side waiting with increasing impatience, judging by the amount of sighing he was doing. I kept looking up at him and saying "Sorry, just one sec" as my struggle continued.

Finally he said, "Do you want me to help you?" I was tempted, Lou, but for him to help me, I'd have to tell him my combination. And according to every adult ever (Mom, Dad, Mr. Smeed, Mr. McCabe, the principal), telling someone your lock combination is the dumbest thing you could possibly do. But here I was, already considering it on the first day of school.

While I was kicking Davis Davis's question around in my head, he got tired of waiting for an answer. "Look, can I just go real quick?" he asked. "I don't want to be late for my next class."

"Okay," I said, even though I was starting to figure I'd be the last person in line for lunch. But I knew I couldn't make Davis keep waiting too; it was getting awkward. I stood up and watched as Davis opened his lock in a blink. As I was marveling at the perfectly arranged contents of his locker (color-coordinated binders, spiral notebooks lined up in size order), I felt a sharp, stabbing pinch on my bottom, followed by a braying cackle.

I was about to come face to face with one of the worst parts of middle school.

# 10. The Gooser

"OUCH!" I yelled as a wave of pain went through half my backside.

"Geez, grow up, Gosley," Davis Davis said with a roll of his eyes.

The cackles continued, and I turned and saw they were coming from a tall, pale boy with pimples on his face.

"Gotcha, Four Eyes!" he said with another cackle. "What were you staring at Davis's locker for, huh, Four Eyes? See something you like in there?"

"I'm just waiting to get to my locker," I said. "And don't pinch me!" I looked around, hoping maybe a teacher had seen what had just happened. But there were only kids in the hallway.

"Keep your eyes on your butt and not on Davis's

locker, and maybe you won't get pinched again, Four Eyes!" he said.

Which of course is completely stupid. How can someone keep her eyes on her own butt? But Ronald Gosley is beyond stupid. He's a mean, pitiful jerk. In fact, he's actually kind of famous for those things, but what he's most famous for is pinching girls' backsides, also known as goosing. Does he care that there's a person attached to the butt that he's pinching? He does not. It's like what Mom says about how she doesn't like commercials where men *objectify* women, or just treat them like they're objects for entertainment. I don't think I got it until I met this kid. It's a stupid game for him, leaving bruises on the female backsides of Meridian Middle School. (Crazy, right? That someone could get away with pinching people so often that he'd actually become famous for it? I know that would never fly at Starling Elementary. Ronald Gosley would have landed in the principal's office the first time he pinched another kid. But grown-ups aren't always with you in middle school the way they are in elementary school. Jerky kids can get away with stuff they never would have when they were younger. Sometimes you can't depend on teachers to save the day.) These were all things I didn't think about until later. From the way Ronald Gosley laughed, and the way Davis Davis and the other kids walking by barely reacted, it seemed like this was just a part of middle school I had to put up with, like strict teachers and tricky locks.

Anyway, because pinching girls' butts is his favorite pastime (and also because of his last name), I would soon find out that Ronald Gosley is known as the Gooser. He would eventually get what he deserved from another kid. A girl, actually. More on that later.

But I've already said too much about him. Up next: lunch.

# 11. The crusher

Lunchtime. First day of middle school. Potentially one of the most terrifying moments of your life. Not terrifying like jumping off the high dive at the pool, or like the dog in Dad's apartment building that snarls at us whenever we see it in the hallway. This is worse.

First-day-of-middle-school lunch terror feels more like you've just landed on a new planet where all the other aliens know exactly what to do, and you are totally confused by their customs. Some of the aliens may look familiar, but even they seem to know the right things to do: what food to get, who to talk to in the lunch line, where to sit once you're ready to eat.

So I tried to pretend I was one of the aliens. I noted what food most of them were getting (Nachos Fiesta) and avoided the ones they were avoiding (school pizza). I didn't know the kid in front of me—or the kid behind me—in line. (Surprisingly I wasn't the last one in line; I guess I wasn't the only kid with first-day locker struggles.) But I acted like that was no big deal and picked at my fingernail while I waited. Once I had my tray, instead of looking around frantically for a table the way I felt like doing, I scanned the room calmly, as though I had agreed to meet someone and I just needed to confirm her location.

And the trick worked! No one gave me weird looks or told me I was doing the wrong thing, and as I scanned the room, I even saw a reasonable place to sit.

Alone at a table by the wall, sitting under a banner that said DARE TO BE REMARKABLE!, was Amber Travers. Amber and I had been friendly since first grade. We were usually at each other's birthday parties, and sometimes we carpooled together to Girl Scout meetings—things like that. She wasn't someone I told all my secrets to, but she was generally okay. Like I said, it was a *reasonable* place to sit, not the ultimate dream seat. (The ultimate dream seat would have been at a table with Layla, but I knew that wasn't going to happen again until high school. I wondered how Layla's first lunch at Parkwood was going. Did she have anyone to sit with?)

Amber spied me at about the same time I spied her, and she started waving. When I walked over and put my tray down at her table, she said, "Oh, thank God. I didn't want him to think I was sitting alone."

"Who?" I asked.

"Shh!" she said, even though I thought my volume level had been perfectly normal. "Sit down!" She said it urgently, like there was a rock flying at my head.

I sat. "Who are you looking at?" I asked, because Amber hadn't made eye contact with me since she first saw me. Her eyes were focused somewhere off in the distance.

"What is that on his T-shirt?" she asked, either not hearing my question or ignoring it completely. "A picture of a little girl looking in a window? That's kind of weird, isn't it?" She did a little nervous laugh.

"*Whose* T-shirt?" I asked. "Amber, what are you talking about?"

I turned around. There were so many kids behind us, I couldn't be sure where Amber was looking. Then I noticed Nick Zambrano putting his tray down at a table with three other boys from Starling. The flannel he'd had on this morning was tied around his waist now, so I could see what he'd had on under it: a black T-shirt with a picture of a little girl in a white dress looking through a window in an old door. You'd know it from Mom and Dad's CD collection, Lou. It was one of the ones they both wanted to keep when Dad moved out. Mom said he could take it if he made a copy for her.

"You mean Nick's shirt?" I asked.

"SHHH!" she hissed. "Stop looking at him! Turn back around!"

"Okaaay," I said, turning back toward her. "Yes, it's a girl looking in a window. It's the cover of a Violent Femmes album."

"Violet what?" she asked.

"*Violent* Femmes," I said. "It's a band. My parents like them. They're pretty good, actually."

"Do you think Nick likes them too?" she whispered.

"I guess," I shrugged. "If he's wearing the shirt."

"Can you text me the name of that band later?" she asked. (There is a strict rule at Meridian Middle about not bringing phones to class, and leaving them in your lockers during the school day.) "I don't have a pen with me right now."

"Okaaay," I said again. "Amber, do you have a crush on *Nick*?"

"A crush?" She sighed. "More like an obsession. But you can't tell anyone."

"Okaaay . . ."

"Stop saying that!" she said.

"Sorry, sorry. I guess I just never thought of Nick as

someone anybody would have a crush on. Or an *obses-sion* with."

"Don't you think he's so different than he was at Starling?" she asked. "I didn't see him all summer, and now he's taller. And I think his voice is deeper."

"I don't know," I said. "I saw him at the pool a bunch over the summer. He seems the same to me."

"You saw him *at the pool*?" Amber asked me in a voice that started in a high pitch but ended in a fierce whisper. "What was that like?"

"It wasn't *like* anything. I was mostly with Layla, and he was with Jason and Mekhai. We all played Marco Polo a few times."

"You played *Marco Polo* with him?" Amber asked, as though I'd said we'd gotten engaged.

"Well, yeah. We were at the pool."

"Tell. Me. Everything." Amber ordered. "Starting with what he looks like without a shirt on."

Ew. That was it. We had been warned during our puberty talk with the school nurse at Starling last year that girls generally mature more quickly than boys, and that girls might start showing "romantic inclinations" sooner. But I would hardly call the way Amber was act-ing "mature" (or "romantic," for that matter). In fact, she was officially weirding me out.

"Amber, you're officially weirding me out," I told her. I had only had about three bites of my Nachos Fiesta, but my appetite was gone. "I'm gonna go practice opening my lock." I admit it was a pretty lame excuse, but I don't know if Amber even heard a word I was saying. Besides, as I've established, I did need some lock practice.

"Oh, you're leaving?" Amber's tone was surprisingly disinterested, considering she had been frantic for me to sit with her five minutes ago. She was still looking at Nick. While pretending not to look at him.

"Yes. Lock practice." It sounded even lamer the second time I said it.

"Can you wait a minute and watch me throw away my food scraps?" Amber asked. A request that made "lock practice" sound really important.

"Why would I do that?"

"Because I have to walk past Nick on my way to the trash can, and I want you to watch and tell me if he looks at me."

"Thanks, but I'll pass," I said, deciding that I'd clear my tray at a different trash can on the other side of the cafeteria.

I turned to make my escape from Amber, and that's when I ran into the next person I would meet in middle school.

# 12. The Other Alien

"Hey," said a short girl with long brown hair and a narrow, serious-looking face. "You're Augusta, right?"

"Yeah," I said, feeling a little awkward because I had no idea who she was.

"We played soccer together," she said. "I'm Sarah Novak."

"Oh right," I said. "On the Hurricanes."

I remembered now. Sarah was on my soccer team in second grade. She was quiet but friendly. We used to blow dandelion seeds in the soccer field together, and we had the shared distinction of being the only two kids on the Hurricanes who scored goals against our own team. (It was very confusing for a second grader. Why do they have to switch the two teams' goals halfway through the game? Now you know why I didn't play soccer again after that year. I'm guessing Sarah didn't either.)

"Yeah," she said. "Did you finish your lunch already?"

"Sort of." I didn't feel like explaining why Amber and her crazed hormones had made me lose my appetite after two bites of nachos.

"Oh, okay." She looked disappointed. "I couldn't find a good place to sit, so I'm taking my lunch outside."

"We're allowed to do that?" I asked.

"Yeah," she said. "My brother told me. Josh went here until last year; now he's in high school."

It was sunny out, and so warm this morning that Dad had tried to convince me to wear sunscreen. (I'd said no. Did not want to start middle school with an extra-shiny face.) But it was definitely one of those first days of school that seem especially cruel because it still feels like summer. Sitting outside with Sarah didn't sound like the worst way to spend the rest of my lunch period.

"I can still hang out with you if you want," I told her.

"Okay, good." Sarah smiled. "I think it's this way to the courtyard."

We walked down a short hallway to a door I hadn't

noticed before. It opened onto an interior courtyard with a brick pathway and a few stone benches. The courtyard was overgrown with weeds, and long strands of ivy trailed over the pathways. But I could tell it had been cared for once: honeysuckle flowers grew on a trellis on the opposite side, and a gold plaque on the wall near us read IN LOVING MEMORY OF MRS. JACKIE SISTRUNK.

"Wow," I said. "I didn't know this was here. I can't believe no one else is out here."

"Yeah," Sarah said. "Maybe it's more crowded during seventh- and eighth-grade lunch. But most sixth graders don't know about it yet. It'll probably get crazier here later in the year." (She would turn out to be right about that, but not in the way she meant.)

We only had about fifteen minutes left in lunch period, and it went quickly. She told me everything she knew from her brother about the teachers I had. (Some things were no big surprise: for example, that Mr. Smeed was really boring. But other information he had was unexpected, like the fact that Ms. Tedesco used to be an actress.) She also told me that Ms. Barakat, the teacher I was going to have for language arts after lunch, was "goofy, but nice."

I asked Sarah if she knew anything about Mrs. Sistrunk, the person the courtyard was named after.

"Only that she was everyone's favorite teacher," she said. "And she led a club that gardened in the courtyard. But she died a few years ago."

It made me sad to know that someone had once loved this courtyard and cared for it, and now she was gone and the courtyard was overgrown. How had everyone else let that happen?

I wondered something else: Where were Sarah's friends from Minter Elementary? Who had she eaten lunch with there? Wasn't it weird that she apparently had no one but me to eat with here? I almost asked her, but then I realized she might be wondering the same thing about me. Maybe she had a Layla of her own who'd also wound up at a different middle school. Maybe she hadn't seen anyone safe to sit with either. Maybe she was also feeling like an alien.

# 13. Your favorite teacher

I don't know if you'll have a favorite teacher in sixth grade, Lou, but I hope you do. You probably won't know yet on the first day. I didn't. And I was convinced no one could ever beat Mr. Singer from fifth grade anyway. He made up songs to teach us state capitals. He took us on a field trip to the beach. He let us team up to answer questions about stories in the news, and the winning teams got candy (like whole chocolate bars, not just weird little dinner mints). He actually made school fun almost every day. Everyone loved him so much that kids *and* parents cried at the surprise party we threw for him at the end of the year when he left teaching to go to journalism school.

Anyway, at first I thought my language-arts teacher, Ms. Barakat, was a little goofy, like Sarah had said.

She was all kinds of asymmetrical: her blouse was only partly tucked in, and half of her skirt hem was coming apart. Even some sections of her hair hung down lower than others (but not in an artsy, intentional way—more like she'd had a bad haircut).

But Ms. Barakat has turned out to be one of the best parts of sixth grade, which has come in handy because I have people like Addison Aldrich and Heidi Carruthers in my class. And they have *not* been the best parts of sixth grade. More on that later.

The first day of school Ms. Barakat asked us to write her a letter telling her what we hoped would happen in sixth grade. This assignment raised a lot of questions in the class.

Heidi Carruthers: "Can it be something like 'I hope I meet Spoiler Alert?'" (Spoiler Alert is Heidi's favorite boy band. As you know, I think their music is pretty terrible.)

Natalie Daniels: "Can it be 'I hope we don't have any homework'?"

Addison Aldrich: "Can it be 'I hope we read Shakespeare'?"

Eric Hewson: "What about 'I hope the school burns down'?"

Ms. Barakat said yes to all these. (But she did add,

"Although I hope you'll give careful consideration to the implications of what you're hoping for," when she answered Eric.)

"Definitely stretch your brains a little," she said. "That's what we're here for. If you want to include any wishes that I might be able to help come true—like reading Shakespeare, or maybe going on a field trip to see a play—then that would be great. But the other wishes are interesting too, and will help me get to know you.

"Oh! Which reminds me," she said, "you need to get to know me too. So it's only fair for me to share my letter with you all." She tapped the Smart Board, and this letter appeared (I remember it pretty well because she wound up printing it out and posting it on a bulletin board):

*Dear Sixth Graders,*
*Welcome to Language Arts! Here are a few of the things I hope for all of us this year:*

*1. If you already love reading and writing, I hope that in my class you will discover books and poems that will expand your universe and make you love words even more than you already do.*

2. *If language arts is not your favorite subject, I still hope that in this class you will meet a book or a writer who speaks to you and makes you think!*
3. *I hope we discover more about the things that connect us to each other and to people throughout time.*
4. *I hope you will not hesitate to ask questions or offer insights.*
5. *Finally, I hope that middle school for you can be a time of getting to know yourself and finding your village.*

Heidi raised her hand. "What do you mean, 'finding your *village*'?" she asked.

"Your people," Ms. Barakat explained. "The ones who make you feel at home in your own skin."

Addison, Marcy, and Heidi exchanged a look that said they already had a village and were also quite comfortable with their skin, thank you very much.

I looked around and wondered if I would ever have a village at all. Or feel comfortable in my skin. Half the time lately, I didn't even feel "at home" in our actual home. Either of them.

In my letter to Ms. Barakat, I wrote:

*I hope for a good year with good grades and not too much homework. And I hope you're right about finding a village. And feeling at home. We'll see.*

I signed my name and folded the letter twice before dropping it in the wire basket on her desk as I left the room.

## 14. The math teacher

Walking to the next class on the first day, I braced my-self. Who was I going to find in here? The Huggers? Natalie and her dance friends? Some other kids who already had their village? And what about the teacher? Would it be a man or a woman? Would he or she slam the desks with a golf club, give us weird jobs, or say things to embarrass me?

So it was a relief when I walked in and the first person I saw was Sarah. And there was an empty seat beside her.

"Hey, sit here," she said when she saw me. I was glad she said it right away so I didn't have to ask if she was saving the seat for someone.

"What was your class last period?" I asked her.

"Band," she answered. "Are you in band?"

I just said that I wasn't. I didn't tell her that I wanted to be in band, but that an instrument wasn't really in Mom and Dad's budget this summer, between renting Dad an apartment, and getting new furniture for it, and buying us an extra everything (jackets, boots, jeans, sweaters) because the family therapist said that would "ease the transition" (oh yeah, they also had to pay the family therapist) . . . well, I just kind of sensed that it wasn't the right time to ask about renting a trombone. Or two trombones, come to think of it. So I was stuck with gym as my elective. Joy.

"How was language arts?" Sarah asked. "What'd you think of Barakat?"

"She seems okay; she made us write about things we hope for this year."

"Oh yeah, I have her first period. We did that too. I wasn't sure what to say, so I made up something about field trips. Who was in that class with you?"

I told her about Addison, Marcy, and Heidi. "Do you know them?" I asked her.

"I know Heidi," she said. "We were in the same ballet class when we were younger and we got to be friends."

"Oh," I said, kind of surprised. Heidi didn't seem like someone Sarah would be friends with. "Are you guys still friends?"

"Not so much."

I wanted to ask more, but I wondered if the story of Sarah's friendship with Heidi was something she'd rather not talk about, sort of like me and the reason I wasn't in band. Besides, class was starting.

As for the math teacher, Ms. Rice . . . she's the kind of adult I imagine a lifeguard would grow up to be. Or, like, a really good athlete who also volunteers to build houses for homeless people. She is super confident, a little tough but also kind, and of course really, really good at math. All things I'm not so sure I'll ever be.

# 15. The renegade

My next class was gym. Since I figured Mom and Dad wouldn't let me take band and I had to do the gym elective instead, it's fair to say I was not exactly looking forward to it. In fact, I was dreading it. I recognized a few of the kids in gym from classes earlier in the day. One of the Huggers was in there. Also Jason Cordrey. But no one I wanted to squeeze next to when the gym teacher, Ms. Lewis, told us to line up on the first bleacher and sit down. The first bleacher was about twenty kids wide . . . and there were twenty-five of us in the class. Squish.

I wound up smushed between the lone Hugger and Jason, who pretended he didn't know me even though we'd been in the same class together four times since preschool. Fine. I guess I was pretending not to know him either. He was at the end of the row, practically falling off the edge.

The last kid to sit down was a girl I didn't know who I recognized from homeroom. She didn't hurry to get beside a particular person. She didn't squeeze her way between people, or try to perch at the end. In fact, she didn't even sit in the front row at all. She strolled over to the bleachers, examining her fingernails like they had something written on them, and sat in the third row, two bleachers behind everyone else.

"Excuse me," Ms. Lewis said, clutching her clipboard to her chest and pointing. "You in the third row. What's your name?"

The girl glanced up from her fingernails and looked at the bleachers in front of her. She bobbed her head a couple of times, apparently counting to see which row she was in. She looked up at Ms. Lewis.

"Me?" she asked.

"Seeing as how you're the only person in the third row," Ms. Lewis said, "yes. You."

"Oh. I'm Quincy."

"Hello, Quincy. Welcome to physical education. I asked you all to please sit on the *first* bleacher. Not the third." Ms. Lewis reached up to her blond ponytail and gave it a little flip through her right thumb and fore-finger, like she was making sure it was still there.

"There's no room there," Quincy said.

"All your other classmates managed to find spots."

"But they're all squished together. What's the point?"

"The *point,* Quincy, is for me to find out how well you all follow directions. It seems I've already learned something about you."

I glanced at Quincy out of the corner of my eye. She didn't move or apologize or blush or do any of the things I would have done.

No, Quincy leaned forward to a boy in the front bleacher and whispered, "Do you think we need pens in here? I forgot my pen."

"*Quincy!*" Ms. Lewis's eyes were open so wide I could see the whites all the way around her blue irises. "We are not talking and we do not need pens and we are SITTING IN THE FIRST ROW."

Quincy looked up again. "I guess I'm just not sure why." Her voice was perfectly calm, completely differ-ent from the tone Ms. Lewis was using.

"So you think you should all be able to just sit wherever you want, even though this is my class?" Ms. Lewis's voice seemed tighter, somehow, than it had when we first walked in.

"Well, if there's no room where you want us to sit, then sure," Quincy answered.

Ms. Lewis narrowed her eyes. "Everyone except Quincy, please go to the locker rooms and choose the lockers you will use for the year. I know you don't have gym clothes with you yet today, but next time you will, and I will expect you to change quickly. So spend some time practicing opening and closing those locks. Quincy, you wait here for a moment to speak with me."

Great. Locks again. I fell in with the rest of the class as they split into two separate groups walking toward the doors at the far end of the gym (one with a BOYS sign above it, the other with a GIRLS sign).

Even though it was only the first day of school, the locker room already smelled like dirty socks. The lockers were all bright orange, kind of like the jumpsuits people in prison have to wear. I put my backpack on the bench in front of an open locker at the end of a row and pulled out the lock Mom had bought me for gym. Not surprisingly, most of the other girls already had their locks on their lockers and were spinning the dials like tops as they chatted with each other. I, on the other hand, was alone with my closed lock and my clumsy fingers.

"Do you need help?" a voice beside me asked. I looked up and saw Quincy standing at the locker beside mine, already putting an open lock on it. I guess it hadn't taken long for Ms. Lewis to say whatever she had to say to her.

Quincy didn't seem to notice that I hadn't answered, because she kept going. "Here, I'll show you a trick," she said, reaching for my lock. "What's your combination?"

Again, someone I didn't know offering to help with my lock. And this time, she was blatantly asking for my combination.

"Oh, let me guess," Quincy said when I hesitated. "You don't want to tell me. You're afraid if you tell me your combination, I'll break into your locker after school and steal your smelly gym clothes."

"I just don't think we're supposed to . . . ," I started to say.

"Whatever, I'll show you on mine," Quincy said. She started spinning her dial. "Okay, so my combination is eleven, fourteen, twenty-five. So I go to eleven first, then back around to fourteen, then leave it. Next time I come in here, I just have to turn it to twenty-five, and then it'll open. It makes it way faster."

"Well, I guess Ms. Lewis would be happy about that," I said.

"Eh, who cares about her?" Quincy shrugged. "It's mostly a good trick for your hall locker if you're ever running late to another class. And I always am. Also, have you heard about that Gooser kid who pinches girls on the butt? You don't want to turn your back too long anyway, with him lurking around."

"Yes!" I said. "He got me this morning!"

"Yeah, he's the worst," Quincy said. "My sister warned me about him. If he ever does that to me, I'll punch him."

"Hasn't anyone ever reported him?"

Quincy shrugged. "My sister says he always denies it. I guess he has to get caught in the act." She pointed at my lock. "Okay, try the trick now."

I got my lock open and put it through the loop on the locker door, then turned the dial past the first two numbers of the combination.

"Okay, it's set," I said. "I'm gonna try that on my hall locker too. Thanks."

"Sure," Quincy said.

I didn't know what to say to her next. I was actually hoping Ms. Lewis would come in to get us so I wouldn't have to think of things to talk about with Quincy. I started picking at a white spot on my fingernail.

"That spot won't come off," Quincy said. "It's under your nail, on your skin. My mom says they're just calcium deposits, but my sister told me they show how many boyfriends you have. I have millions of 'em.

Look." She held her fingernails out so I could see. Sure enough, almost all her nails were dotted with tiny white spots. I just had one. Which was one too many, according to Quincy's sister's theory.

"I don't have any boyfriends," I said.

"Maybe you *do* and you don't know it yet," Quincy said. Then she laughed. "Whatever—my sister's dumb. But it's fun to count the spots anyway.

"So how come you're in here and not in band?" she asked.

I gave the short answer. "I didn't think my parents would let me do band."

"Mine neither," she said. "They said I don't stick with things like that. So now I'm stuck in gym with stupid Ms. Lewis."

Just then the locker-room door swung open to reveal Ms. Lewis with a clipboard and a serious face.

"Time for some stretches, girls," she announced. "Next time you'll change into your gym clothes. And you'll also be working much harder in gym." She looked straight at Quincy as she said the last part. It was unclear whether she'd heard Quincy call her stupid.

Either way, Quincy didn't seem concerned. She turned, rolled her eyes at me, and called, "Let's stretch, ladies!" as she led the way out to the gym.

...

By the time I got to my hall locker after gym at the end of the first day, Davis Davis was already long gone (and thankfully, the Gooser was nowhere in sight either). I opened my lock on the third try (an improvement), dumped the books I didn't need for homework, and reached for my phone on the top shelf. I had seven missed messages.

One from Mom:

> *I hope you're having a great first day, honey! Text me when you get home.*

One from Amber:

> *OK tell me again the name of the band N likes?*

Another one from Mom:

> *Also, don't forget to walk Iris.*

A second one from Amber:

> *N means Nick, in case you didn't know. OK DELETE THIS NOW! But also tell me what the band is called. Purple something?*

A third one from Amber:

*And don't tell him I asked you about it.*
*But just tell me the band name, OK?*
*RU getting these texts?*

One from Layla:

*Gus! Text me!* 🐕

Finally, one from Dad:

*Hey Gus—I just realized I forgot to tell you*
*that you were supposed to go around to the*
*back door this morning. Oops. Hope your*
*day was OK anyway!*

Layla's text had come in about fifteen minutes ear-lier; Parkwood Middle lets out for the day before Me-ridian does. I texted her back, but she didn't respond for a while; my guess was she was on the bus, avoiding mo-tion sickness. (Layla gets really carsick. Remember the time she went to Longwood Beach with us and we had to pull over on the way home so she could throw up?)

I walked home by myself. I didn't see anyone I knew. Well, that's not true. I saw Marcy and Addison walking together, but I slowed my pace so I wouldn't be near them. So let's say I didn't see anyone I *wanted* to walk with.

I was tired. Really tired. *Bone tired,* as Dad would say. And that was just day one.

# 16. Layla, the Parkwood Middle School superfan

Yes, Lou, I realize that technically Layla was someone I already knew. In fact, I'd known her since we were tiny. Or at least I thought I knew her.

The Layla I *thought* I knew was one of the calmest kids ever. Like, there could be a spider on her hand and she would slowly walk over to a tree and let it crawl onto a branch. That kind of calm.

And she was definitely never someone who got worked up about sports, or games . . . or school spirit. At Starling Elementary, whenever we had a theme dress-up day (you know, Pajama Day, Funny Hat Day, School Colors Day), she would always gripe about it on the way home from school the day before. "Ugh, do we *have* to dress up tomorrow?" she'd ask me. "What's the point?"

It's not like I was a major gamer for dress-up days.

I mean, some kids would come to school in homemade hats with giant feathers on them, or temporary tattoos in school colors. I never did any of that stuff. But I did appreciate the chance to stay in my pajamas and get a few extra minutes of sleep on pajama days.

Maybe that's why I couldn't figure out the meaning of all the panther emojis at the ends of Layla's texts on the first day of school:

*Hey! I'm home!*

*How was the first day?*

*Can you come over?*

I texted her back:

*OK, will come over after snack. What's with all the panthers?*

She responded:

*Yay! Panther is the Parkwood mascot. Cute, right?*

That was my first clue that Layla's first day must have been much different than mine was. I wasn't even sure what the Meridian mascot was. An armadillo, maybe?

I texted Mom: *Going to Layla's*. She was still at work and you were at after-school. I know that bugs you, Louie, that I get to go home on my own this year and you still have to go to after-school. I know you think that means I eat all the snacks I want and watch more TV than I'm supposed to. You're right. I do.

But I also have to unload the dishwasher and wash lettuce for the dinner salad and fold laundry all the time. So it's not like it's all a big party.

Anyway, when I got over to Layla's, she was sitting on the steps, tapping away at her phone.

"Buzz Bust?" I asked her. (You know how Layla was always playing Buzz Bust last summer; it was her favorite game.)

She hadn't even noticed me standing there.

"Huh? Oh . . . no," she said. "I'm texting with Jocelyn."

I peered over her shoulder and saw Jocelyn's last text, which consisted only of an LOL emoji and—big surprise—a panther.

"Who's Jocelyn?"

"Oh, she goes to Parkwood," Layla said. "She's in my math class, and we sat together at lunch. She's so funny. She was doing these imitations of our teachers at lunch; we were all cracking up."

"Huh." I couldn't really think of anything to say to that, since I didn't know any of her teachers. Or Jocelyn.

"Soooo . . . how was it?" Layla asked me. "What's Meridian like?"

"I guess it's okay," I said. I gave her the first detail

I could think of. "My science teacher has a bat named Lorenzo."

"Ooh, cool!" Layla was impressed. "Is it a fruit bat or a vampire bat?"

"Um, no . . . ," I answered. "It's a baseball bat. He walks around and bangs it on your desk if you aren't paying attention."

"Oh. That sounds kind of scary."

"Well, not as scary as a vampire bat," I pointed out. Layla laughed. I was glad she still thought I was funny. (Take that, Jolly Jocelyn!)

"Oh, and we get to eat outside if we want," I told her. "In a courtyard."

"We have to eat in the cafeteria for now," Layla said. "But starting in October, if we get our parents' permission, we're allowed to leave school at lunch and go to Filippo's or Pop's!"

I know you're obsessed with Chicken Shack, Lou, but as far as I'm concerned, Pop's and Filippo's are way, way better. Pop's has awesome sandwiches and old-school pinball machines, and Filippo's really is the best pizza place in town. They're both about a block away from Parkwood. And they are undeniably way better lunch spots than the overgrown courtyard at Meridian. No contest, really.

"Well, that's amazing," I said.

"Right?!" Layla was hiding her excitement about as well as I was hiding my envy. "And the principal stood by the door in a panther costume welcoming everyone to school today. AND all the sixth graders got the cutest little stuffed panthers and panther T-shirts. I forgot mine in my locker, though. Ooh, also I got a top locker! Did you?"

"No." I was secretly relieved that I didn't yet have to endure seeing Layla's cute new panther on top of all the other amazing stuff she was telling me about Parkwood.

How could Layla and I have had such ridiculously different first days of school? I'd spent the day feeling like an alien, and she seemed like she already *belonged.* Like she already had her village. How could she be so sure about middle school when I was convinced I would never figure it out?

It was around then that Mom called to tell me that you guys were home. I told Layla I had to go, and she said she'd ask her mom about doing a sleepover so I could stay longer and see all her panther stuff. *(Yes, please, to the sleepover; no, thanks, to the panthers.)*

And not long after that was when I shuffled through the door and gave you guys my first "It's fine, whatever" when you asked about my day. Maybe now you understand why.

# 17. Syd the tomato kid

The weather stayed warm for a while, so Sarah and I kept eating lunch in the courtyard. And she was right: eventually other kids started discovering it too. Most came in with friends, like Nick and a boy I recognized from my social-studies class, who always sat by the crab apple tree and threw crab apples. They had contests to see who could hit a target they'd drawn on the wall in chalk.

One kid, Elaine Farley, always sat alone with a book and a ham sandwich. Sarah told me Elaine had gone to Minter, but was very quiet and she didn't really know her that well.

And then there were kids who knew about the court-yard but would never consider eating lunch there. For example, Addison, Marcy, and Heidi, who walked by the courtyard door one day on their way to the bathroom. They peered in for a second and started whispering to each other, but not quietly enough that I didn't catch bits of what they were saying.

"Who are you talking about?" Heidi asked.

"You know," Addison said, shrugging and half trying to appear as though she weren't talking about us. "The one with glasses." When Heidi still looked clueless, Addison hissed, "Come on—she's the *only* one with glasses."

There was no point in looking around the courtyard. Obviously they were talking about me. They did that a lot: look at people and whisper about them. I guess that day it was my turn. Even though I knew this whisper game was their regular hobby, it still felt like a spotlight was shining right on me. I stared into my chip bag and waited for them to move on. As they started walking away, I heard Heidi giggle and say, "Do you think she'll wear her glasses to the *dance*?"

And Addison answered, as though she knew us so well, "Ugh, they're all so weird. They probably aren't even going."

The Sadie Hawkins dance wasn't happening until

November, but Heidi had joined the planning committee and talked about it every morning in homeroom. It was clearly very important to her.

···

Do you remember the date of my eye doctor appointment last year, Lou? I do. It was November third. I probably wouldn't remember that, except for the fact that something big happened after it. Have you ever noticed that the ordinary parts of a big day suddenly become much more memorable long after the big thing happens? Like the way Grandma Dotty says she remembers what she was wearing, and what the weather was like, and what they had for breakfast the day President Kennedy was shot? Because of all the terrible things that happened that day.

Anyway, November third wasn't just the day of my last trip to the eye doctor; it was also the day Mom and Dad told us that Dad was moving out and they were getting divorced. I know your parents getting divorced isn't the same as the president dying, but you see what I mean. It marked the day on my brain. That's how I remember when my eye appointment was.

Up until then, November third had been a pretty good

day. Mr. Singer had let us watch *March of the Penguins*, and Layla had brought her mom's shortbread cookies to share at lunch. *And* I didn't have to go to after-school because Mom left work early to take me to see Dr. Sherman.

Nothing about the appointment was out of the ordinary. Dr. Sherman asked how school was, did my eye exam, and said my eyes had gotten a little worse. Then she said, "I know when you were here last year, you asked about getting contacts once you were in fifth grade. Are you still interested in that?"

I was about to yell "YES!" because, as you know, I'd been wanting contacts for what felt like forever, and Mom had said I could get them at my next appointment if Dr. Sherman thought it was okay. So I figured today was the day.

But before the word was out of my mouth, Mom said, "I think we'll need to discuss it more. I'll let you know."

I looked at her. "Wait, what? I thought you said I could get contacts this year."

"I said we'll discuss it later, Gus," Mom said, and she was using that voice that told me I'd better not push my luck, especially not in front of Dr. Sherman.

Mom turned back to Dr. Sherman. "Just the new lenses for today, please."

I brought it up again in the car. "Mom, what was that about? You said I could get contacts this year. I'm going to middle school next year. I need to get used to them before then. I am *not* starting middle school with glasses!"

Mom sighed and told me to stop freaking out, and that contacts were expensive. And then she said something we've since heard her say many more times over the past year: "We just need to think about the money."

So that was weird. I mean, it's not like Mom and Dad were the kinds of parents who bought us anything we wanted all the time. But when there was something they'd promised—something that was a *medical necessity* as far as I was concerned—they never changed their minds and said it was too expensive.

The next weird thing that happened that day was when we pulled into the driveway: Dad was home. Wearing jeans and a T-shirt and raking leaves. Way earlier than he usually was home from work. You were there too, because he'd picked you up from after-school. Then they said they had to talk to us about something. And before long we were hearing their weird reassurances about how it wasn't our fault and we wouldn't have to choose between them.

You know how the rest of that day went.

That's when Mom and Dad had to start spending money on things like the divorce lawyers. And the apartment for Dad. And his furniture. And the extra clothes for the extra "home" for us.

And that's why I started middle school with glasses.

Anyway, almost a year after that eye appointment on November third, I wanted contacts so bad I could taste it. It wasn't just because my glasses start to slip down my nose when I sweat in gym class. Or because they get all fogged up when it rains. Or even because the stupid Gooser called me Four Eyes.

I think it had something to do with what I told you before: the wondering about what other people thought of me. At Meridian, what did I look like to the people I passed in the hall? Every time I looked in the mirror and thought about that, I couldn't even really tell what I looked like to other people, because all I saw was glasses. And judging by what Addison said to Heidi, I wondered if maybe that was all other people saw too.

■ ■ ■

After Addison, Marcy, and Heidi moved on, Nick's friend by the crab apple tree called over to us.

"So, are you?"

Sarah looked at me. "Are we what?" she yelled back.

The boy took a bite of his tomato. (Why was he eating a tomato like it was an apple?)

"Going to the dance?" he asked.

"Why do you want to know?"

"Relax, Sarah, I'm just making conversation," he said. "You should learn how to do that one of these years."

Sarah rolled her eyes. "Just eat your tomato, Sydney." She started crumpling up her lunch wrappers and looked at me. "Are you almost ready to go?"

I looked at the rest of what was left of that day's lunch (cashew chicken). It wasn't exactly tempting.

"Okay," I said. "We can go."

Sarah didn't look at Nick and the other crab-apple-tree boy, Sydney, as we walked past them on our way out. Even when Sydney yelled, "It's been a pleasure dining with you ladies!"

"You know that kid Sydney?" I asked her once we were back in the hallway.

"Ugh, yes," she answered. "And apparently now he wants to be called Syd, but he was always Sydney when we were at Minter."

"I wonder how he knows Nick," I said. "He went to Starling with me."

"Is Nick into music?" Sarah asked.

"Yeah."

"Then that's probably how they know each other. Sydney thinks he's a rock star because he has some lame band that plays in his garage on weekends. Maybe Nick is in it."

"Why don't you like him?" I asked Sarah.

"Who? Sydney?" She shrugged. "He's not the *worst*—I mean, last year I always ate lunch in the art room, and he was usually there too, helping clean brushes and stuff."

"You were allowed to do that?" I asked.

Sarah nodded. "Yeah, we could work on extra art projects while we ate. It was more fun than the cafeteria."

So now I had some idea of what Sarah's lunches were like last year. Maybe she just wasn't a cafeteria kid. Which was fine with me.

"But Syd . . . I don't know," she said. "It's like he's weird on purpose, saying things like 'It's been a pleasure' and eating tomatoes like they're fruit."

"Tomatoes are fruit," I said.

Sarah gave me a little sock in the arm. "You know what I mean."

I changed the subject.

"Do you think I look okay without my glasses?" I asked, and I took them off and looked at her.

"Oh yeah!" she said. "You should get contacts!"

I thought for a second. "Can I tell you a secret?" I asked her.

Sarah nodded, and I told her about That Day. The day of the appointment with Dr. Sherman, the day of the divorce announcement, the day of no contacts. Have you told anyone about that day yet, Lou? Until then, I hadn't.

And then Sarah surprised me.

"Yeah, when my parents got divorced, they worried about money all the time too," she said.

"Your parents are divorced?" I asked her.

"Yeah," she said. "For a while now. Anyway, you need to be proactive."

"What do you mean, 'proactive'?"

"Take charge. Tell them you'll help pay for the contacts."

"I don't have any money."

"Well, then," Sarah said as I put my glasses back on, "you need to find a way to make some."

# 18. The new houseguests (strictly speaking, not people)

By the time you and Mom got home after work and school that day, I had folded laundry, unloaded the dishwasher, walked Iris, cleaned up Iris's poop in the backyard, made a salad, warmed up leftover lasagna, and set the table for dinner.

Mom was wearing her scrubs with *Sesame Street* characters on them, which meant she had worked in the pediatric ward that day. It also meant she was probably in a good mood, because the maternity and pediatric wards are her favorites. On the days she has to work in the emergency room, she is much more tired when she gets home.

So I liked my odds for having a good conversation about contacts. Mom was fresh off a day with cute little kids, and I had done a ton of chores. What could go wrong?

"Well, your sister has lice," Mom said, dropping her keys on the hall table and kicking off her special white nurse sneakers. (Lou, you may remember that you started running upstairs, and Mom yelled, "Uh-uh! Straight to the laundry room! Strip down and then get in the shower!")

"Ugh!" I was grossed out, as anyone is when finding out about a lice infestation, but I tried to stay positive. "Well, on the bright side, I folded laundry, and cleaned up Iris's poop, and made a salad!"

Mom looked doubly grossed out. "Did you wash your hands between picking up the poop and making the salad?"

"Yes, of course!" I said. "I warmed up the lasagna too. Are you ready to eat?"

"First I have to check your head," Mom said. "Sit down and lean over."

Mom put on her reading glasses and started poking through my hair with a pencil. It felt like she was drawing on my head. But I knew better than to complain.

"I guess you're clear," Mom said, although she seemed uncertain. "Can you check me now?" She pulled her hair out of its bun, sat on a kitchen stool, and flopped her head down onto the counter.

This was kind of weird. Last time we'd had a lice scare, I was in fourth grade. Dad had checked Mom's hair that time. It definitely seemed like the kind of thing an adult should do for her, like zipping up her dresses or fastening her bracelets. But there was no other adult here. It was on me.

"You know what you're looking for, right, Gus? Not just bugs, but also little eggs clinging to the hair. Nits." Mom's voice was muffled since her head was resting on her arms. It was probably good she couldn't see me, because I was grimacing as I raked through her hair, afraid that bugs would pop out from behind every strand.

"Okay, I *think* you're clear," I told Mom.

She sat up and sighed. "Thanks, Gus. You're a good egg. No pun intended." She reached up and tousled my hair (and I could tell she was giving it another quick once-over to see if anything was crawling in it). "Now I have to go deal with your sister."

Mom had exhaled a little since she walked through the door. I felt like this was my chance.

"Hey, Mom, before you go upstairs, I wanted to ask you something."

She seemed to tense up again. Not a great sign. "Okay, but can it be quick?" she said. "I have to make sure Louie's using the lice shampoo."

I said the next sentence all in one breath. "Well, I know my appointment with Dr. Sherman is probably coming up soon; and I wonder if this year I can get contacts like we talked about and before you say no what if I help pay for them?"

Mom sighed. "Really, Gus, this is what you want to talk about right this second when I have to get bugs out of your sister's hair and wash all the clothes and bedding in the house?"

"Okay," I said, "but maybe we can talk more later? Did you hear the part where I said I'd help pay for them?"

"With what money?" she asked.

"I was hoping we could figure that out together?" I said. "Like maybe I can find a way to make some money by helping around the house and then pay you back after we buy the contacts?"

"Gus, you are supposed to help around the house anyway," she said. "You are a member of this family and that's what family members do. God knows I don't get paid for helping around the house."

"Okay . . . maybe something else, then?"

Just then you called from upstairs. "Mom! I need help and I'm itchy all over!"

"Gus, I really can't discuss this right now," Mom said, grabbing her hair tie off the table and throwing it in the trash can. (Clearly she wasn't convinced that her head was bug-free.)

So. We both know that "I can't discuss this right now" just means that Mom hopes we will drop the subject, and that if we don't, she'll find a way to say no later. I could see I was going to have to find a way to start making money without her help.

# 19. The Binaca lady

Here's something that happens in middle school that never happened in elementary school: the teachers leave you on your own to work independently a lot more often. For most of the teachers, this means they quietly grade papers while they give you a good chunk of time to read or write or solve math problems.

But with Mr. Smeed, this means he actually *leaves the room*. I don't know where he goes; he always just says, "I need to step outside for a moment. Get organized for your day." Maybe he makes phone calls? Maybe he chats with another teacher? Maybe he has a bladder condition? I'm not sure.

Is Mr. Smeed supposed to leave us alone in the class-room? I don't think so. But let's be honest: homeroom is way more enjoyable when Mr. Smeed isn't in it, so none of us are going to say anything to get him in trouble.

One day Mr. Smeed was gone for even longer than usual.

"Where do you think he goes all the time?" Nick asked me.

"I have no idea. But at least when he's gone he isn't handing me a bunch of papers to file."

"Maybe he's going out to buy more Bianca." Gabe Garrett leaned across the aisle and offered this theory. With his face that close to me, I couldn't help but think that he could stand to use some breath spray himself. "Have you ever noticed he's addicted to that Bianca stuff? He sprays it in his mouth all the time."

"It's *Binaca*, not *Bianca*," Nick corrected him. "Bianca is a girl's name."

"Whatever," Gabe said. "I bet he has a drawer full of it."

"If he has a drawer full of it," Nick said, "then why would he be going out to buy it?"

Gabe had to think about that. "Maybe he just can't get enough. Maybe he goes through a couple of bottles of it a day. I think that stuff has alcohol in it. What if it's like his secret way of getting drunk at school?"

"It doesn't have alcohol in it," Nick said. "My grandma uses it."

"So?"

Now it was Nick's turn to think. I don't know why, but I felt like I had to stick up for his grandma.

"Even if it *does* have alcohol in it," I said, "it's got to be a tiny amount. Not enough to get you drunk even if you used it all day long."

"It does kind of have a burning taste, though," Nick said, and I could tell he was starting to wonder if Gabe was right. "One time my brother and I had a contest to see who could spray the most Binaca on their tongue before it burned too much."

"Who won?" Gabe asked.

"I did," Nick said. "My brother gave up after five sprays but I made it to seven."

Gabe snorted. "That's nothing. I bet I could do at least ten."

"What do you want to bet?" Nick asked.

"Twenty bucks," Gabe answered.

"That's stupid." Nick rolled his eyes.

"I'll do it," I said.

Nick looked at me like I was crazy.

"For twenty dollars?" I said. "Sure, for twenty dollars I bet Gabe can't handle ten sprays of the Binaca."

This was perfect. Twenty dollars would put a good chunk of change into my contact-lens account.

"Nah, that's not enough," Gabe said. "You have to really earn it. It's a contest. Whoever can handle the most Binaca squirts wins."

"What are you guys talking about?" Quincy asked.

Nick told her about the Binaca bet.

"I want in," Quincy said.

"Me too," said Mekhai, who'd overheard Nick's explanation.

I saw a chance to minimize the amount of money I'd be losing if Gabe got more sprays than I did.

"How about this?" I said. "We'll make it like a pool."

"What, like a swimming pool?" Gabe asked. "Full of Binaca?"

"No, a gambling pool. The hospital staff where my mom works do it every year during March Madness for college basketball. Everyone puts ten dollars in a jar and picks which team they think will win. Whoever picks the winning team gets all the money in the jar."

"I'm not paying ten dollars to do this," Quincy said.

"No, you don't have to," I explained. "There are twenty-two of us in here. If everyone puts in one dollar, the winner gets twenty-two dollars at the end."

"That's even more than we first said!" Gabe practically had dollar signs in his eyes.

"Right," I said. "Assuming everyone does it."

"Sounds like a good plan to me," Quincy said. "I'm in." Knowing that Quincy approved of my idea gave me a boost somehow; I knew more kids would get behind something she supported. I should have also known that Quincy's involvement might also increase our odds of getting in trouble, but I wasn't thinking about that just then. I guess I had dollar signs in my eyes too.

"I'm not doing it," Heidi said. "You aren't allowed to gamble at school."

Tyler Peterson didn't look up, but whispered to the robot he was doodling. "Me neither," he said.

"Anyone else out?" Gabe asked. The rest of the class was quiet.

"Okay, then," he said. "Let's see what's in Smeed's secret drawer."

"Wait," Quincy said. "Someone has to be the lookout and make sure he's not coming back."

"I'll do it," Nick said. "But I also want a turn with the Binaca stuff."

"I'll be the lookout when it's your turn," I said.

"All right." Nick started toward the door. "If I see him coming, I'll turn around and say 'necktie.'"

"Why 'necktie'?" I asked.

"Because he always wears neckties."

"Why not just 'Smeed's coming'?"

"Because if he hears me say that, he'll know something's up."

"Oh, and randomly saying 'necktie' isn't at all suspicious?"

"You guys are wasting time," Gabe barked at us. "Just pick one and let's get going!"

"Okay, 'necktie' it is!" Nick said before I could protest; then he bolted toward the classroom door.

Gabe was opening and closing Mr. Smeed's desk drawers and announcing their contents as we all started to crowd around.

"Pens and Post-its."

"Paper clips, stapler, and the comic book he confiscated from Quincy." He tossed the comic to Quincy, who gave a little whoop.

Gabe opened the big bottom drawer and whistled. "The mother lode!" he announced.

I looked over his shoulder. A small plastic basket held four loose bottles of Binaca, and under that were two big unopened boxes with a picture of a smiling blond lady and the words *Binaca! Are you ready?* emblazoned across the top. Printed in the bottom corner of each box was *Quantity: 30 bottles.*

"I was right! He has like a million bottles in here!" Gabe was clearly proud of himself.

"More like sixty-four," I said.

"Whatever," Gabe said again. "There's still plenty for us to do our bet, and Smeed won't even notice any are missing."

I wasn't so sure about that. Mr. Smeed was the most organized person on the planet; he probably had his Binaca inventory recorded on a spreadsheet somewhere. But for some reason, I didn't care. I was too excited about the idea of winning twenty dollars toward my contact-lens fund. And Gabe was being seriously cocky; beating him would be a nice side benefit.

"Okay," Gabe said, pulling a baseball cap out of his backpack and setting it upside down on a table, "if you want to play, put a dollar in here." Kids started rummaging through their own backpacks looking for dollar bills and loose change.

"Also, someone has to be the scorekeeper," he said. "Heidi, since you aren't playing, what about you?"

"I'm not *playing* because you're *gambling*," Heidi said. "So I won't keep score either."

Gabe rolled his eyes.

"Fine," he said. "I'll keep score until it's my turn, then someone else has to count how many sprays I get."

"Okay," I said; then I took a deep breath. "Who wants to go first?"

Four different kids said "Me!" at the same time. I handed a Binaca bottle to Quincy, since she was standing closest to the desk, and said, "Here, you go. And put a dollar in the pool first." Quincy dropped four quarters into the baseball cap.

She sprayed her tongue. "Ooh, it's minty!"

She sprayed a couple more times. "Woo!" she said with a sharp inhale. "Definitely getting spicier."

After two more sprays, her eyes started looking watery, and she waved her hand in front of her face. "Okay, I'm out. It's starting to burn."

"Five sprays," said Gabe as he added a final tally mark beside Quincy's name. "The number to beat is FIVE."

Quincy went back to her seat beside Heidi, who looked at her with narrowed eyes. "Did it make you drunk?" she asked.

"I don't think so," Quincy answered. "I just can't feel my tongue."

Heidi gave Quincy a long, suspicious look before leaning back in her seat and returning to her book, *Anne of Green Gables.*

I handed the tube of Binaca to Mekhai. He also got five sprays before his nose started running and he gave up. The spray bottle continued down the line for a while; most kids stopped at three or four sprays, but Eric made it to seven.

By the time it was Gabe's turn, seven was still the number to beat. We had gone through all four loose bottles in the basket, so he took one of the unopened boxes out of the drawer.

"Time for the Binaca lady!" he said. "Hey, maybe *her* name's Bianca!" Gabe laughed at his own stupid joke.

"Okay," he said. "Here goes nothing." Gabe made it easily through the first five sprays, but after six he started to slow down. After seven he wiped his eyes and said, "Whew!" But he kept going, past eight . . . nine . . . ten. By then his eyes were really watering and he was starting to sweat. He eked out one more spray, dropped the bottle on Mr. Smeed's desk like he was dropping a mic, then pumped his fist in the air. "Eleven!" he yelled, and some of the boys cheered.

"You're up, Reynolds," Gabe choked out. Nick turned around from his post by the door and looked at me.

"Still clear out there?" I asked.

"Still clear," Nick answered. "No necktie."

I took a fresh Binaca bottle out of the drawer. Somehow I couldn't stomach the idea of using the same one Gabe had used. I had to beat his record and make it to twelve sprays. How hard could it be?

I took one spray. Quincy was right; it was minty. Kind of like a blast of one of Dad's Altoids. The second spray was more of the same, but a little sharper. By the time I got to the fourth spray, it was definitely making my tongue feel warm. Spray five: watery eyes. Spray six: runny nose. Around spray seven, my tongue lost feeling. The same happened to my cheeks by spray number ten. Two more to go.

By now some of the kids were chanting my name: "AugusTA, AugusTA, AugusTA." It made something click inside me. I pushed past the burning and the numbness and the tears to pump the top of the spray bottle one, two, three more times, for a total of thirteen sprays of Binaca. Lucky number thirteen.

Everyone but Gabe went wild. "Thirteen sprays! Way to go, Augusta!" Quincy said. I grabbed a tissue from the box on Mr. Smeed's desk, lifted my glasses, and wiped my eyes.

"Not bad, Reynolds," Gabe said. "Now we'll see if Zambrano can beat that."

I grabbed another couple of tissues before walking to the door to relieve Nick from lookout duty.

"Whoa, Augusta, that was impressive," he said, and gave me a clap on the back.

"Ha, thanks," I said. "Everyone has a talent." I stepped inside the doorway and gave my eyes another wipe; they were still really watery.

I could hear the kids around the desk counting Nick's sprays. "One, two, three, four . . ." The counting paused for a second, then continued at a slower pace. "Five . . . six . . ."

I wanted to turn around and watch, but I knew I had to be the lookout. Plus, my eyes were watering so much that I couldn't see very clearly. Which, come to think of it, was a pretty big problem to have when you were supposed to be the lookout.

Whew, my eyes were really stinging. I started to wonder if it had been such a good idea to take thirteen sprays of Binaca. What if I was allergic to it and I didn't know? Could you go blind from using too much Binaca? No, if that were the case, then Mr. Smeed would probably be blind by now. But I doubted he'd ever had thirteen sprays right in a row.

These were the thoughts I was pondering when I heard someone coming down the hall. I tensed up. Was it Smeed? The footsteps didn't sound like they belonged to a sixth grader. I was just getting ready to yell "necktie" when a tall person rounded the corner. It was our neighbor, Rob Vinson.

"Hey, Little Gus! What's going on?" He stopped and looked at me. "Whoa, what's up, Little Gus? Why are you crying? What happened?"

"I'm okay," I said. "I think it's just, um, allergies."

Somehow talking made it worse. My eyes were practically fountains. I started wiping them again.

"Little Gus . . . that looks pretty serious. You should tell your teacher. Whose class is this? Smeed's? Tell him you need to go to the nurse."

"No, it's fine," I said, blowing my nose, which had also started to run.

"I don't think so, Little Gus," Rob said. "Look, here he comes now. I'll tell him."

With watering eyes, runny nose, and the light-headed feeling I always get from impending doom, I turned to see Mr. Smeed two feet away, approaching from the other direction.

"What's this about, Miss Reynolds? Mr. Vinson, where are you supposed to be?"

But we couldn't hear Rob's answer, because it was drowned out by the sound of my entire homeroom cheering and shouting, "Augusta won!"

Mr. Smeed pushed past me to open the door all the way, just in time to see Nick (also with watery eyes) holding a bottle of Binaca, the rest of the class huddled around him, and a baseball cap full of cash sitting in the middle of his desk.

Suddenly my list of symptoms expanded to include a sore throat. But as the door closed behind me, I managed to grimace at my class and cough out a single word: "Necktie."

# 20. The principal

"Let me get this straight," Principal Olin said, looking across her desk at Mr. Smeed. "You stepped into the hall to take an emergency phone call, and when you returned, the students had stolen property, used an unapproved substance in school, and started a gambling ring?"

"That's right, Ms. Olin," Mr. Smeed said.

Nick gave me a look again, the same look he had given me the first time Mr. Smeed had lied and said he'd been just outside the classroom on his phone.

"And the entire class was involved?" she asked.

"All but Ms. Carruthers and Mr. Peterson," he answered.

When Mr. Smeed had first entered the room and seen

everyone chanting around the hat full of money, it was clear he didn't know where to look first. There was a lot to take in: the money, his open desk drawers, Nick holding a bottle of Binaca, everyone except Heidi and Tyler out of their seats, and me, wiping my eyes and coughing. Since I was standing behind him, it might not have been obvious that I was involved, except for the fact that he'd heard people yelling "Augusta is the winner!" He decided to start there.

"The winner of what?" he bellowed. "Just what is going on here?! Mr. Zambrano, what is that in your hand?"

Nick dropped the Binaca and started coughing. His eyes were watering almost as much as mine were.

Mr. Smeed took in the room full of watery eyes and coughing kids. "Were you ALL using my Binaca?" he thundered.

"Not all of us," Heidi said in a voice just above a whisper, not looking up from her book.

"Who, then?" Mr. Smeed asked. We were all quiet. The volume level in the room was exactly opposite what it had been five minutes earlier.

Just then Assistant Principal Wyatt happened to walk past. Great timing.

"Mr. Wyatt!" Mr. Smeed called into the hall. "Perhaps

you can help us here." He explained the situation as though he were describing a grisly crime scene (using phrases like "egregious breach of decency" and "time to unmask the perpetrators").

Mr. Wyatt ate it up. "Well, there's one easy way to find out who the guilty parties are," he said. "Line up." We looked around the room, not sure what he had in mind. "I said line up!" he yelled. "Against the back wall. Every last one of you."

"Now," he said, after we were all in a line, leaning against the back wall. "Breath test. One by one."

Was he serious? He was really going to conduct a crime-scene investigation by making all of us breathe on him so he could see if we'd used Binaca? Yes, Lou. Yes, he was.

Mekhai was first in line. "Mr. Curry," Mr. Wyatt said, "I want you to look up at me, open your mouth, and say 'Hello, Henry!' using as much breath as you can." He put extra emphasis on the *H*'s as he said it.

"Who's Henry?" Mekhai asked. "Is that your real name?"

"No, Mr. Curry, but it is a name that begins with an *H,* and it makes it easier to detect Binaca on your breath when you say it!" he explained. "And there is no need for you to continue anyway, Mr. Curry, because I could smell the spray right away when you said 'Who's Henry?' Clearly you were involved. Take a seat."

"Ms. Hiller, you're next," Mr. Wyatt said, moving on to Quincy. "Hello, Henry."

Quincy repeated it, and so it went down the line, the entire class saying "Hello, Henry" one by one as Mr. Wyatt smelled our breath and sent us to our seats.

The craziest thing was, it worked. When Mr. Wyatt got to Heidi, she said, "Hello, Henry," and he said, "No, just regular toothpaste. Thank you, Ms. Carruthers." And when it was Tyler's turn, Mr. Wyatt sniffed, looked up in the air for a moment, and then said, "Onion bagel for breakfast?" Tyler blushed and nodded. "Very well," Mr. Wyatt said. "You're in the clear too."

The bell rang just as the investigation was concluding, and Heidi and Tyler were allowed to go to class. But Mr. Smeed escorted the rest of us straight to Principal Olin's office. I briefly wondered who was going to be in charge of Smeed's first-period class. Wasn't he worried that they would get into the Binaca too?

"So how did this get started?" Principal Olin asked. "Whose idea was it?"

I figured I was doomed then. I mean, Gabe was the one who had first suggested a bet, but it had been my brilliant idea to turn it into a gambling pool. Those things I remembered. The rest of it was a blur. And I was suddenly feeling a bit light-headed again, wondering if people get sent to jail for starting gambling rings.

Gabe and I made eye contact for about a quarter of a second; then we did what the rest of the class was doing and stared at the floor. No one said anything.

"This is exactly what happened when I asked them," Mr. Smeed said. "No one will talk. *I* say, if they're all so good at not talking, maybe they'd like a week of silent lunch!"

"All right, then," Principal Olin sighed. It seemed like she wasn't thrilled to be taking Mr. Smeed's suggestion, but couldn't think of anything else. "For the rest of this week, this homeroom class will have assigned seating during lunch, and during that time you are to eat your lunches and not talk to each other, or to any other students. The cafeteria monitors will record and report the names of any students who violate the silence."

Out of the corner of my eye I saw Nick mouthing "violate the silence" as he continued to stare at the floor. He was probably thinking it sounded like a song lyric. But I knew that for the rest of that week, there wouldn't be much to sing about.

# 21. Your old best friend's new best friend

"Really, Gus? A *gambling ring*?" News of the Binaca incident had reached Mom and Dad via a call from the principal's office in the middle of their workday. Mom had just gone on break after hooking up an IV for a kid with a bad stomach bug. Dad was in the middle of a sales call with a big advertiser for the radio station. They weren't happy.

"What ever gave you such an idea?" Dad asked, rolling the pizza cutter through one of the pepperoni pies he'd picked up on the way over from work. (They had sent you upstairs to finish your homework, Lou, so they could yell at me in private. I could tell you wanted to hang out and hear what was going on. I saw your shadow in the stairwell, which is why I knew you'd be there when I hissed, "Go upstairs, Louisa." And rolled my eyes when you popped your head around the corner and whispered, "Okay, but later just tell me what a gambling ring is!" I know I still haven't told you. It's never going to be my favorite subject.)

After you went upstairs, the questioning continued. Technically this wasn't supposed to be a "Dad" night, but you know how he and Mom had decided occasional family dinners were still important, especially when there was something to discuss. Like one of us being in trouble. Sometimes I'm glad they still get along pretty well. This was not one of those times.

"I got the idea from Mom's work," I said. "You know how they do that March Madness pool every year. I didn't know it was *illegal*."

"It's not illegal when adults do it," Dad said. Then he looked at Mom and made a quizzical face, like he was silently asking, *Wait—is it illegal?* Mom closed her eyes and shook her head, which either meant *No, it's not illegal* or *It possibly is somewhat illegal but we are supposed to be focusing on yelling at Gus right now.*

"But I still don't understand *why*," Mom said. "Why was this something you wanted to do?"

I couldn't believe they were so clueless. "Because I need money!" I said. "Because I'm sick of wearing glasses and you said I could buy contacts last year and then you guys split up and didn't want to spend money on anything ever, and then I tried to ask you about it again the other day and you didn't even want to talk about it because Louie had lice, and it seems like you guys are always distracted by *something,* so when this chance to make money on my own came up, I took it." I took a deep breath.

"Okay," Dad said. "I admire your initiative." Mom shot him a look, and he gave her a little hand raise that meant *Hear me out.* "But this is not the way to go about it. Maybe we can think of other ways for you to make money. In the meantime, go get your sister for dinner. Mom and I need to discuss next steps."

*Next steps* meant what they were going to do to punish me. As I went up the stairs, I heard Dad whisper to Mom, "Our little high roller," and they both started laughing. I was annoyed that they were making fun of me, but I was hoping that maybe it meant they were in a good mood and I'd get a lighter punishment.

I was wrong.

■ ■ ■

"Hand over your phone," Dad said after we'd finished the pizza and you'd gone back upstairs to do more homework.

"What? Why?"

"That's your punishment," Mom said. "No phone for a week."

"A *week*?" I said. "No way! I need my phone. Take something else away. How will I get in touch with you guys if I need you?"

"You'll do what we did when we were your age," Dad said. "Have the school call us. Or use the home phone if you're here and we're at work."

"But you guys have us split between two different houses! What if someone needs to call me?"

"Give people both of our home numbers," Dad said.

That was such a dumb answer. What was I supposed to do, pass out my parents' home numbers in the hall at school just in case someone wanted to call me during the next week? People I knew hardly even called anyway. Everyone texted. And what about when I wasn't even *at* home?

"What if—"

Mom beat me to it. "If you are somewhere other than school or home, you can ask to borrow someone else's phone if it's an emergency. But let's just hope for an uneventful week; how's that sound?"

It sounded terrible. I needed my phone. My best friend

didn't even go to my school. I had to be able to communicate with her. Which reminded me . . .

"I actually told Layla I'd text her today. Like right now."

"Why do you have to text her *like right now*?" Dad asked.

I did a big sigh. "*Because* we want to have a sleepover and we need to figure out when. We can't do it any old time like we used to because now you guys are split up and I live in two different places and I have to *plan*."

"You know you're welcome to have Layla sleep over here or at my apartment," Dad said.

"But I don't want to do that," I said. I didn't want to hurt Dad's feelings, but I thought his apartment was pretty boring. It had a pool, but that was closed for the season. And since you and I share a room there . . . well, it's not the best for sleepovers. Not to mention that it just would feel awkward to take a friend there. If Layla and I hung out at our house with Mom, it would almost feel like old times before the divorce, like when Dad was on a business trip or something. But if we did a sleepover at Dad's . . . I don't know; it would feel like the divorce was this big obvious thing hanging in the air, on everyone's minds even if we weren't talking about it. Ugh.

I took a deep breath. "I just want to sleep over at

Layla's house," I said. "And now it's all complicated since we can't do school nights and you guys have to take turns with us on weekends."

This time Mom held her hand up when Dad started to talk. "Okay, Gus," she said. "You can talk to Layla about planning a sleepover. But don't use your phone. She lives a block away; just walk over and see her. You know, also like you used to do."

I clenched my fists and bit my tongue to keep from making an "AAARGH!" sound. I also made sure to close the door softly on my way out, because I knew if I was accused of throwing more "attitude" at Mom and Dad, I could lose my phone for even longer. Maybe it was good that I couldn't text at that moment; I needed to get out of the house and see Layla. She'd make me feel better.

●●●

Layla did not make me feel better. When I got to her house, her dad answered the door. That wasn't the best start because, well, you know how Mr. Perkins has always made us nervous because he's so quiet and also perpetually grouchy? Seeing me at his doorstep at eight o'clock on a school night didn't help that.

"Augusta?" Mr. Perkins is the only person in our neighborhood who doesn't call me Gus. "What are you doing here so late?" He leaned out the door and looked up and down the street like he suspected I was playing a prank on him.

Mr. Perkins wasn't inviting me in, so I was standing on the front step, but I could still hear music coming from upstairs in the house, and smell something baking in the kitchen.

"I need to ask Layla about something," I said. "And I can't . . . find my phone to text her." I *almost* said I couldn't *use* my phone, but no way did I want to get into the whole Binaca/gambling ring/phone punishment story with Mr. Perkins.

Then Mrs. Perkins popped into the doorway. As usual, her level of grouchiness was the opposite of Mr. Perkins's.

"Gus!" she said, like she was a talk-show host introducing a famous guest. "Hello, stranger—how have you been?"

"Okay," I said. Suddenly I felt really tired. I wasn't sure which parent I felt less like talking to right now: grouchy Mr. Perkins or chatty Mrs. Perkins. "I was wondering if I could talk to Layla for a minute. Is she here?"

"Of course she's here," Mr. Perkins said. "It's a

school night. She lives here. Seems like she's the only kid in town who *is* where she belongs right now."

What did he mean by that?

"Oh, Terrence." Mrs. Perkins swatted at him and rolled her eyes. "Gus, come on in. Layla's upstairs with her friend Jocelyn from school. Run on up and see them."

Jocelyn. If I were younger, like you, Lou, I probably just could have turned and run home and gotten away with it. Mr. and Mrs. Perkins would have just shaken their heads like *What a kooky kid*. Or if I were older, like Mom, maybe it wouldn't have been weird for me to say something like "It sounds like they're busy; I'll come back another time" and gracefully turn and walk back down the front path.

But I'm not in elementary school. And I'm not an adult, or even a teenager yet. I'm in the middle. And I couldn't think of what to do, so I just said, "Uh, okay," and started walking toward Layla's room.

As I climbed the stairs, my stomach did that flippy thing it does when you're approaching the top of a hill on a roller coaster and you're wondering how bad the drop is going to be. But roller coasters are way more fun than this was.

Layla's bedroom door was closed, and I could hear

laughing over the music. They were listening to the score of Layla's latest favorite Broadway musical, *Scribble*. I knocked on the door.

"YOU MAY ENTER," Layla said in this ghoulish voice we use sometimes when we're goofing around. I'd always thought of it as one of our special private jokes. As I heard another kid cracking up in response, I realized I was wrong.

I pushed the door open slowly. "Hey," I said when I saw Layla sitting on her bed.

"Oh. Gus. Hey," she said. Not exactly the warm welcome I'd been hoping for. "I thought you were my mom. We baked cookies, and she said she'd bring them up here when they're done."

She looked like the wicked queen in a Disney movie. Her eyelids were caked with glittery magenta shadow, and she had dark streaks of red on her cheeks. The girl sitting on the floor in front of Layla's bed fiddling with her phone—Jocelyn—looked the same, except her eye shadow was green.

"Oh, hey, this is Jocelyn," Layla said, like she'd just realized she should probably introduce two people in her bedroom who were complete strangers to each other. "Jocelyn, this is Gus."

Jocelyn looked up from her phone. "Hey," she said, then went back to scrolling through a song list.

"What's up?" Layla asked. "You don't usually come over this late on a school night."

It was true; I didn't. But why was it weird for *me* to visit this late on a school night, and not Jocelyn? Were they becoming friends like the Huggers, who spent every minute together and had school-night sleepovers? When they'd known each other for, like, a month, and Layla and I had known each other for most of our lives?

Suddenly I couldn't imagine asking Layla when she wanted to have a sleepover. Not in front of Jocelyn.

"I just wanted to tell you I can't text right now, so if you need anything, call our home phone."

"What happened to your phone?" Layla asked.

"Long story."

"Ooh, here it is!" Jocelyn tapped the screen of her phone and jumped off the bed to turn Layla's speakers up. "This is the song I wanted you to hear!"

A chorus of peppy teenage voices started bubbling out of the speakers. I knew that sound from somewhere.

"Wait . . . is this Spoiler Alert?" I asked. Layla hated Spoiler Alert as much as I did. We always made gagging sounds and skipped to the next song any time we heard them. I'd been wanting to tell her about how they were Heidi Carruthers's favorite band, because that was evidence of how awful the Addison-Heidi-Marcy trio was. It was one of the topics of conversation on my mental list for the sleepover that I now wondered when we would ever have.

"YES!" Jocelyn squealed. "I love them. My mom said maybe we can go see them next time they tour. I would DIE."

I looked at Layla. She was just looking at the floor, tracing a flower petal on her rug with her big toe. I knew she didn't dare make eye contact with me. I couldn't believe she wasn't saying anything. I mean, *Spoiler Alert?* UGH.

"Okay," I said. "Well, I'm gonna go do homework."

"Okay, see ya," Layla said.

As I was heading down the stairs, she called out, "I'll text you later."

I was so eager to be gone from there that I didn't bother turning around to remind her that she couldn't.

# 22. The kid who talks to his lunch box

Silent-lunch seating in the Meridian cafeteria is no joke. After the Binaca incident, Mr. Smeed consulted with the lunch monitors and they made a chart that reflected which kids they thought would be least likely to enjoy each other's company in the cafeteria.

Our cafeteria tables are small, and usually they're pushed together to make longer tables where big groups of kids can sit. But for silent lunch, the cafeteria staff separate these little tables and put just four kids—two girls and two boys—at each one. I guess they figure that will be less fun for us than a table of all boys or all girls? This shows you how grown-ups think.

At any rate, on the first day of assigned lunch, it was clear that the Map of Misery was a success. All up and down our row, you could see kids approaching their designated tables with feelings ranging from uncertainty to dread to outright terror.

My particular table, table 4, was empty. I wasn't sure which would be worse: being the last person or the first person to arrive at your table. I plunked down my bag lunch and waited to see who my cellmates would be. I figured they must be in line to buy school lunch, because I was still alone, debating whether to start eating or pretend to focus on something else, like my shoelaces. Or the one tiny white dot on my fingernail.

But just then another lunch-from-home person approached my table. It was Tyler Peterson, the only kid besides Heidi who hadn't been part of the Binaca challenge. He was carrying a red lunch box with a picture of the Beatles on it, and he set it down across from me on the table.

"Why are you sitting here?" I asked him after looking around quickly to make sure no lunch monitors saw me "violating the silence." "You didn't get in trouble."

He didn't say a word, or even look at me. Just pulled out his chair and plunked down his lunch box.

Here's something that's important for you to know, Lou: kids at Meridian Middle do not carry lunch boxes. They just don't. They either buy school lunch or they bring brown bags from home like I do. So the fact that

Tyler had a lunch box was already weird. We had been at Meridian long enough by now for him to notice that no one else carried a lunch box anymore.

But that's not even the weirdest part. And the fact that he was sitting at a silent lunch table when he wasn't even being punished wasn't the weirdest part either (although that was still pretty weird). Since I'd barely heard him speak in homeroom, and he wasn't saying anything to me now, I started to think maybe he hardly talked at all. I was wrong.

As soon as Tyler sat down, he opened his lunch box, took out a sandwich, apple, and potato chips, and set them on the table. Then he used his thermos to prop up the lid of the lunch box (the part with the Beatles picture on it), turned the lunch box around . . . and started talking to it. In a really bad British accent.

"'Ello, lads," he said in a loud whisper. I looked behind me to see who he was talking to. No one was there. I turned back around as he was opening his potato chips and saying "Crisps from Mum again today, eh?" He definitely wasn't talking to me. He didn't even seem aware I was there. And then I realized he was talking to the Beatles. The Beatles on his lunch box. And this continued for the rest of the week we had assigned lunch seating. Even after the other people at our table arrived, Tyler kept talking to his lunch box. He kept it to a whisper, and he piped down any time a lunchroom monitor strolled by, but he never stopped for more than a few minutes.

By the end of silent-lunch week, I figured out that the Beatles were the only people Tyler wanted to talk to, and he didn't really care who knew about it. And since he didn't care about talking to other kids, he didn't care about silent lunch, even when he hadn't done anything wrong.

There are just so many kinds of people in the world.

# 23. The serious lunch monitor

The other two kids at my assigned table were Nick and Quincy. I guess this was a relief. I mean, it could have been way worse. I know it seems like it shouldn't matter who you're sitting with when you can't even talk to them, but somehow it still did. Silent lunch would have been truly unbearable sitting across from Gabe shooting milk out of his nose. (Just shows how little Smeed knows about us; if he'd really wanted to torture me as he designed his seating chart, I would have been sitting with Gabe.)

Here's something I noticed about silent lunch: It makes you feel like an animal in a zoo. Everyone looks at you, and you wonder what they know about you, and what they're thinking. There was no poster beside our "habitat" saying:

Mr. Smeed's homeroom class, male
and female. In captivity because of a
gambling ring started by one of the
females, Augusta Reynolds.
Eats turkey sandwiches, pizza,
cookies, and Nachos Fiesta. Do not
talk to them. Cannot speak under
threat of detention.

But there didn't have to be a sign. Everyone knew why we were there, eating in pitiful silence. Word about the gambling ring had spread quickly, and all kinds of crazy rumors had sprung up around it. Like that we were drinking vodka in class. And that there was a thousand dollars on the table when Mr. Smeed walked into the room. Sarah asked me after school one day if it was true that Nick had gotten third-degree burns on his tongue from the Binaca. (He had not.)

I could tell what people were thinking as they walked past our row of tables. Some people, like Sarah, looked sympathetic. (I actually felt bad for Sarah too; she said that since I had to sit with my homeroom, she was either going to be stuck with some kids she knew from Minter who just traded stickers at lunch . . . or she might just read a book by herself in the courtyard like Elaine Farley.)

Other people had faces full of pity when they looked at us. On the first day of silent lunch, Ms. Tedesco and I briefly made eye contact as she walked past our row on her way to the salad bar. She gave me a sad little smile and looked away. I wondered if she was thinking, *She probably became a delinquent because her parents got divorced.*

And then there were the people who seemed happy to witness our punishment. Specifically Addison, Marcy, and Heidi, who at some point had also allowed Amber into their lunchtime crew. (I guess Amber had gotten tired of me ignoring her texts about Nick and moved on.) The four of them wore matching smug smiles as they sat in the row beside ours. They also had matching silver hoop earrings, matching silver bangle bracelets, and matching silver ballet flats. The Silver Sisters.

All week long I got to hear their conversations during lunch. Most of the time it was deadly dull. For example:

Addison: "What if I always wore my hair in a side ponytail like it was the eighties?"

Heidi: "And, like, leg warmers and pink mascara and all that?"

Addison: "No, just the side ponytail. And I acted like it was normal."

Marcy: "That's hilarious."

Amber: "You should totally do it."

Sometimes it was slightly more interesting:

Amber: "If you could go to the dance with anyone, who would it be?"

Heidi: "Probably Rob Vinson?"

Addison: "Ugh, I don't think there's anyone in this school I'd want to go with."

Marcy: "Yeah, you're right."

Amber: "Yeah, me neither." (Hmm. Apparently Amber's Nick crush was over. Either that or she didn't want to admit it to the other Silver Sisters.)

And other times their conversation was clearly about me. I could tell because it would be preceded by one of them making a not-so-subtle glance my way. For example:

Addison: "If you had to wear glasses, wouldn't you just make your parents get you contacts instead?"

Marcy, Heidi, and Amber in unison: "Yes, totally."

Or:

Heidi: "It's so weird that you used to be *friends* with her."

Marcy: "We weren't really *friends*. She was just in my class."

I wanted to yell, "*You* were the one who followed

me everywhere when *I* wanted to be left alone! For a whole year!" But I didn't. And not just because I wasn't allowed to talk. Something told me that it wasn't safe to point out the truth with those three. Silence was easier.

Nick and Quincy heard these conversations too. When the Silver Sisters talked about ponytails, Quincy looked at me and rolled her eyes. Same when they talked about dates for the dance.

When he overheard the glasses conversation, Nick pointed to his eyes and held out an open hand to me. He wanted me to hand him my glasses. I took them off and gave them to him. He put them on and stuck his tongue out, then hooked his fingers behind his ears and wiggled the stems of the glasses to make them bounce up and down on his nose. He looked ridiculous, and Quincy and I started to laugh.

"This doesn't sound like silent lunch to me, girls!" A lunch aide wearing a name tag that said MS. VANWICKLE was walking by our table at exactly that moment. Of course, no one had ever noticed Tyler talking to the Beatles, but one laugh from Quincy and me got us in trouble.

"You'd better take this seriously." Ms. Vanwickle

lingered by our table for a minute, presumably to make sure we were being sufficiently serious.

The Silver Sisters looked over and smirked again. But as Nick slid my glasses back to me and Quincy tried to stifle her giggles in a fake cough, it was suddenly easy to ignore them.

# 24. Benjamin Franklin

I know you were excited for Halloween this year, Louie.
You decided around April that you were going to be a
marshmallow; then you changed your mind and said
you were going to be a tube of toothpaste. Then a vampire. Then Dorothy from *The Wizard of Oz*. By the time
October finally rolled around, you were back to marshmallow. At that point you were talking about your costume all the time, and I could tell you were disappointed
that I had way less interest. I remember the day you
gave up. We were both sitting at the dining-room table
doing homework and you said, "Gus, if I'm being a
marshmallow, maybe you could be a chocolate bar and
we could dress Iris up like a graham cracker and together we'd be a s'more." And I just rolled my eyes and
said, "No thank you." That was when you sighed and

muttered sarcastically to yourself, "Well, *that* was a good conversation starter, Louie." And Mom overheard you and came in to give you a quick little hug.

Anyway, I'm sorry, Lou. In the weeks since then, I think I've understood a little more about how much you want us to do things together. And you should know that my Halloween wound up being pretty boring. Embarrassing, even. Here's the deal with Halloween in middle school: As far as I can tell, it's really only cool to care about it during certain hours, like at night when you get free candy. You're *allowed* to wear your costume to school . . . but almost no one does. There's no class party or costume parade around the schoolyard. No parents come to take pictures of how cute you all look. The only kids I saw wearing costumes were Natalie Daniels (ballerina, of course) and Tyler Peterson (Beatle, of course; I don't know which one).

I was wearing a new jacket that day. Well, new to me. It was Mom's old navy blue coat from when she was in high school that has those cool gold hook-and-eye buttons down the front. Usually I only wear it when we have to dress up for something, but my regular coat still had mud all over it from when Iris had jumped on me with happy doggy greetings—and filthy doggy paws— the day before.

So I grabbed Mom's old coat on my way out the door, and didn't remember until I was almost at school that it was Halloween. Not that I would have done anything differently; it's not like I worried anyone was going to think this jacket was some kind of costume. But then someone did.

"Oh!" Ms. Tedesco squealed when I walked into social studies. (I was still wearing the jacket because her classroom is always cold for some reason.) "Were you inspired by your trip?" she asked.

I thought she was just asking a general question about our DC trip again, since that was her favorite subject.

"Um, yes?" I figured that was the safe answer. It was not.

"I knew it!" She clapped her hands together and did a little jump. "Even though he's really associated with Philadelphia, not Washington. But of course he was still one of our finest founding fathers!"

I truly had no idea what she was talking about. I just nodded at her and slunk over to my desk.

After the bell rang and everyone was settled, it started to become more clear.

"Okay, class, happy Halloween!" Ms. Tedesco beamed. "*And* may I extend a very warm welcome to our very own . . . Benjamin Franklin!"

She held out her hand like she was introducing the Queen of England (or, well, Benjamin Franklin). And her hand was extended in my direction. I turned around to see who she was talking about. The only person behind me was Syd, using his pencil to carefully shade the spaces in the letters printed on his notebook cover. I turned back around.

Gabe Garrett had swiveled in his seat and was facing me. "Are you supposed to be Benjamin Franklin?"

"Me? No!" I looked up and realized that Ms. Tedesco was, in fact, directing her gaze at me. As was the entire class.

"Oh, you're not?" Ms. Tedesco looked brokenhearted. "I just thought with that jacket, and your hair looks wavier today . . . and of course, the glasses."

Of course. The glasses. I needed contacts. I needed money. I needed to get a job.

Unbeknownst to me, Mom was already on the case.

# 25. Your boss

"I've been thinking," Mom said as we folded towels together the Thursday night of silent-lunch week (which was also the day after Halloween).

"I can have my phone back?" I asked.

"No. You still have three days until that punishment is over. But I've been thinking of what you said about wanting to buy contacts. And I might have another way you can make money. You know, apart from being a gambling kingpin." Mom gave me a sideways glance, and I think I saw a smirk behind the bath towel she was folding.

"Oh." I'd been hoping she'd say "Dad and I feel bad, and we'll buy the contacts for you after all!" But I guess that was too much to wish for, considering the week I was having.

"Okaaaay," I said. "What is it?"

"You know Dr. Chen at the hospital?" I did. Dr. Chen is a neurologist. She specializes in helping people with brain problems. She is also one of Mom's favorites at work. Mom always says some of the doctors don't listen to the nurses or spend enough time with the patients, but Dr. Chen isn't like that.

"Well," Mom said, "she just had a new baby and she's on maternity leave. Her husband went back to work, and she wants someone to play with their four-year-old daughter, Ama, while she rests or gets some time with baby George. Just a couple of afternoons a week."

I never thought I'd get a job in sixth grade. I figured that would be a high school thing. But Mom said she was my age when she started working as a helper for a family on her street with little kids.

I wasn't so sure. I mean, babies and little kids can be cute, but I didn't want to change any poopy diapers. Mom said that was fine; we could discuss that with Dr. Chen. So I agreed.

Dr. Chen's house is on one of those streets our family has always called a "secret road," but the roads aren't really secret; they're just marked with PRIVATE ROADWAY signs and are only meant to be driven on by the people who live there. When you were little and you fell asleep in the car, Lou, we would drive around town looking for all the secret roads while you slept. Those long drives were the only way Mom could get you to take a nap.

Most of the houses on the secret roads are big, with shady yards and porches that wrap around their sides. On our long drives while you were sleeping, Mom and I would make up stories about the people who lived inside them. Like "I bet that family owns a unicorn named Martha Washington" or "I think the family who lives there lights all their lamps with fireflies."

Mom always says those car rides were the best way to get me to talk to her. I'd tell her about my friends in preschool, or my imaginary friend Gritzy, or the things that scared me. (Back then, my biggest fear was that pirates would break into our house and steal my toothbrush.)

Once the stuff that scared me got realer, it was harder to talk about. Like when Dad spent a week at Uncle Keith's house without us, and nothing like that had ever happened before, and Mom let us sleep in her room with her every night, which she never did on school nights. And once during that week I woke up in the middle of the night and heard her crying, but I pretended I was still asleep. I wanted to ask her if they were about to get a divorce, but I didn't because I was afraid of what the answer would be (turned out I was right, of course).

But I was glad Mom kept taking us for drives on the secret roads, even after I stopped talking to her so much. Once in a while she still got me to play our little game ("I bet that house is owned by a family of gophers!"), and I could tell that made her happy.

So when Mom hooked me up with the mother's helper gig with Dr. Chen and I found out her family lived on a secret road, I was pretty excited.

Of course, as we pulled up to the house the first time I helped there, Mom was making all kinds of goofy references to our game, like "Now you'll find out if they have indoor polo grounds!" and "You have to tell me if they slide up the banister like Mary Poppins!"

I shushed her. "*Mom*. This is my first job. Please be normal, okay?"

Thankfully Mom clammed up when we got out of the car. And she left as soon as she'd said hi to Dr. Chen, so she didn't get past their foyer. I knew she'd ask for a full report when I got home.

The truth is, the house is kind of fancy. They have a big spiral staircase, and windows that go from the floor to the ceiling (plus a round window with colored glass in the stairwell). But it's also cozy, and there are lots of signs a four-year-old lives there, like finger paintings and toys all over the place.

I got to see most of the house before I saw Ama. That's because she was hiding from me. But she was also trying to spy on me, so every time her mom and I rounded a corner, we'd hear little feet running away on tiptoe, and sometimes catch a glimpse of long dark braids disappearing around the next bend in the hallway.

Dr. Chen seemed a little embarrassed. "Ama, Augusta came here just to play with you!" she kept calling. But I remembered what it was like to be little and feel nervous around a new person. It was funny to think that Ama probably thought of me as a grown-up and was hiding, the way I used to get nervous and shut myself in the linen closet when Mom and Dad had friends over.

I thought of a game Grandma Dotty used to play with us when she visited. The next new room Dr. Chen showed me was a bathroom, and I stood in the doorway and said loudly, "Oh, *this* must be Ama's room!" I heard a giggle and a high-pitched "No!" from down the hall.

Dr. Chen caught on fast. She opened a hall closet door, saying, "This is where we keep our towels," and smiled at me. I knew that was my cue. "Oh, so *this* must be where Ama sleeps! On all these soft towels!" Again, laughter and "No, no!" floated around a corner.

The third time proved too much for Ama to take. Dr. Chen opened a door at the end of the hall and said, "This is the master bedroom." I responded with "Wow, this is such a big bed for Ama! She's so lucky that this is her room!"

And with that, a little zip of yellow and orange with two long braids sped past us. She ran into the room beside the master bedroom, a sunny yellow room with a rainbow painted on one wall, and jumped onto a bed with a canopy and a quilted bedspread.

"*This* is my room," she announced. "See?" She pointed to a wall that had the letters of her name hanging on it in big wooden letters.

"Ohhhh," I said. "Well, that makes more sense. This is a way better place to sleep than a closet! So your name is Ama, and my name is Augusta."

"Does Gusta start with *A*?" she asked me. "My mom said it starts with *A*."

"Yes," I said, ignoring the fact that she'd actually just left the *A* off. "Augusta starts with *A*. Just like Ama."

And from then on we were friends. Ama started introducing me to all her stuffed animals and didn't even notice as her mom slipped back downstairs.

# 26. Sadie Hawkins

By mid-November, it seemed like almost every conversation at Meridian was about the Sadie Hawkins dance.

The Monday before the dance, in language arts, Eric Hewson was the first one in the classroom after lunch, and he started writing a list of songs on the small whiteboard Ms. Barakat has labeled WOYM: WHAT'S ON YOUR MIND? We're allowed to write anything we want there as long as it's not rude or offensive; usually it just says things like *I'm sleepy* or *Weekend!* Once in a while someone throws Ms. Barakat a bone and writes something thoughtful about current events or one of the books we're reading (like *Why do you think Stacey in* Roll of Thunder, Hear My Cry *is friends with TJ?*).

Today Eric had written *Dance Songs* across the top

of the WOYM board and listed five of his favorites in orange. Other kids were going up and adding their own to the list in different colors (including, of course, three Spoiler Alert song titles written in pink by Heidi).

"Okay, I know everyone's excited for the dance," Ms. Barakat said. "So take a couple of extra minutes to write your song suggestions. If you want, I can take a picture of the board and text it to the teachers on the dance committee. Because I'm *sure* none of you have your phones with you right now, right?" She gave us a knowing look as half the class sweetly chorused "Right!" back at her. And Heidi added, "I'm on the dance committee, Ms. Barakat, so I'll also write the songs down and make sure everyone sees them!"

"Thank you, Heidi—that's helpful in case my old brain forgets." Ms. Barakat gave her a little smile.

I wanted to add my favorite dance song to the list. You know what it is, Lou: "Blister in the Sun" by the Violent Femmes. Remember how Mom and Dad used to listen to that album on long car trips? And they'd make sure to always play "Blister in the Sun" when we stopped for lunch, so when we got out of the car they could say "Dance break!" and we'd hop out and dance off all our wiggles while the song played?

But I didn't add any songs to the list. I doubted

anyone in the class had even heard of "Blister in the Sun" (of course Nick would have, but he's in a different language-arts class), and I didn't feel like answering a bunch of questions, or dealing with Addison's eye rolls at more evidence of how weird I was.

Once the last song request had been added and people were settled at their desks, Ms. Barakat read us "The Road Not Taken" by Robert Frost. It's a poem about a guy who goes for a walk in the woods and decides to hike on an overgrown path instead of the one everyone else uses. Right when she got to the line that says "I shall be telling this with a sigh," Ms. Barakat stopped and sighed herself. I assumed she was just being dramatic, because she does kooky stuff like that sometimes, but then I noticed she had closed her poetry book and was staring at Addison, Heidi, and Marcy, who had their heads together, whispering.

Ms. Barakat smoothed the back of her hair, took her glasses off, and gave her neck a little rub. She never loses her patience, but I've noticed that she does this hair-smoothing, neck-rubbing move when it seems like she's trying not to yell. Kind of like the way Mom takes a very deep breath when we're fighting (but then sometimes Mom still yells anyway).

It seemed like a full thirty seconds before Addison,

Heidi, and Marcy noticed that the class had ground to a halt and stopped their whispering. Since the rest of the class had already quit talking, we all heard the end of Heidi's last sentence: ". . . and let's all wear cowgirl boots to the dance!"

Ms. Barakat sighed again. "Okay, folks, I think I'm going to try a road less taken myself today. I feel like we won't give Mr. Frost the attention he deserves while our minds are elsewhere, so let's talk about the dance. What do you want to say about it?"

It was the quietest the class had been all year. Most of us *did* want to talk about the dance. A lot. But with each other, not with a teacher.

"Come on," Ms. Barakat said. "This is probably the only chance I—or most other teachers, for that matter— will give you to talk about this in class. So speak up! Any questions?"

"Okay, I have one." Eric Hewson looked around. "Who's Sadie Hawkins?"

"Well." Ms. Barakat took a deep breath. "She wasn't a real person. She was a character in a comic strip. Hang on . . . let me see if I can find a picture." She went to her laptop and did a quick search.

"Here we go." An image popped up on the Smart Board. It was a rough black-and-white drawing of a pitiful-looking girl with a giant nose, bumps all over her face, and a braid that stuck straight up into the air.

"UGH!" Most of the class—especially the boys—gasped like their eyes were burning.

"Yes, well," Ms. Barakat said, "Sadie lived in a place called Dogpatch, and it seemed that everyone in town shared your opinion of her. But her father was rich and powerful, and he was determined to find her a husband. So he announced that every unmarried man in town would have to run in a race."

"And the winner would marry Sadie?" Eric asked.

"No." Ms. Barakat sighed again. "The loser. Her father knew no one in town wanted to marry her, so he was treating her as a punishment, not a reward."

It made me think of Mom, and what she says about commercials that objectify women.

"And either way, he was treating her like she was a thing," I said, without even realizing I was speaking out loud.

"That's right." Ms. Barakat nodded at me.

"So what does that have to do with a dance where the girls ask the guys?" Eric asked.

"What do you all think?" Ms. Barakat asked.

"I mean, for the dance, it's like the girls are in charge," Mekhai said. "But Sadie wasn't in charge; her dad was."

"It's like the boys are being forced to dance with the girls," I said. "Just like some guy was forced to marry Sadie."

"But we don't have to dance with girls who ask us if we don't want to," Eric said. "Wait—*do* we?"

Ms. Barakat smiled. "No, of course not. But it is interesting to think about where customs like the Sadie Hawkins dance come from. I'm glad you asked about it, Eric." Eric leaned back in his chair and stretched, like he was pleased his work was done for the day.

Ms. Barakat looked like she was about to open her poetry book and go back to Robert Frost, but she paused and looked at us. "Do you all have any questions about that?"

"Do you mean, do we have any questions about why our school is having a dance that's named after this awful story?" I knew my out-loud voice was working now, and I was okay with that. Something about the way Ms. Barakat was looking at us made me feel like it was safe to say what I was thinking.

"That's one question." Ms. Barakat smiled at me.

"Yeah, but . . . whatever," Heidi said. "I mean, it's just for fun, and it's not like anyone has to go if they don't want to. Who cares what it's called?"

"And that's another question," Ms. Barakat said.

"Maybe we should care, though," Mekhai said. "I mean, that story is *harsh*."

"That's what I'm thinking," I said. Having Mekhai back me up made it easier to keep talking. Until I looked over at Addison and saw her make a super-prissy pinched face and mouth *That's what I'm thinking* to Marcy, who started cracking up.

"Addison, did you have a thought to share here?" Ms. Barakat asked.

"No," Addison said, straightening up in her chair but clearly still proud of herself for making Marcy laugh.

Ms. Barakat looked at her for another few seconds, then put her reading glasses back on.

"Okay, well, I think it's almost always the case that more thoughtfulness is a good thing," she said. "And I like the way some of you are thinking."

Then she finished reading the poem, about how taking the less-traveled road made all the difference.

# 27. Charlie

Late that Friday afternoon, when I heard Mom approaching the front door I suddenly remembered I was supposed to have taken spaghetti sauce out of the freezer. I got up from the sofa where I'd been lying down and texting with Sarah and scrambled to the kitchen. You were having a sticker-trading session and dinner at Clarissa's house.

"Hey, Gus," Mom said. She glanced at the sofa, and I wondered if she could tell I'd just been lying there. "Texting with Layla?" she asked.

"No, Sarah." I hadn't texted Layla much since I'd gotten my phone back, and I hadn't heard from her many times either. Once or twice she'd send me something dull like *UGH! Hate math!* but there wasn't much to say to that other than *IKR?* It was like neither one of us knew how to act after the awkward Jocelyn meet-up.

"Oh . . . weren't you guys supposed to be planning a sleepover?"

"Who, me and Sarah?"

"No, you and Layla."

"Oh. I don't know. That was a while ago. We kind of forgot about it."

Mom didn't push further, either because she could tell I didn't want to talk about it or because she was suddenly preoccupied with the rock-solid bag of frozen spaghetti sauce on the kitchen counter.

"When did you take this out of the freezer?" she asked, trying to smush the bag around in her hands to see if any part of the sauce was in liquid form.

"When did I take what out?"

"Gus. This spaghetti sauce."

"Oh. A while ago?"

She gave me a look. "I'm going to go upstairs to shower and change. Dump the sauce into a bowl and nuke it, and put some water on to boil for pasta. Please."

When Mom came back downstairs in jeans and a sweater, the sauce still had frosty blobs in it, even though

I'd kept taking it out of the microwave and hacking at it with the handle of a wooden spoon the whole time she was in the shower.

"What are you doing to that poor spaghetti sauce?" Mom asked.

"I'm stirring it."

"Looks more like you're murdering it. Let's just see what we can salvage for now," she said. "I'm hungry." Mom tipped the bowl and let the liquid part of the sauce pour over the pasta, then she put the rest back for another round in the microwave.

"So you know this is your weekend at Dad's, right?" she asked after we sat down, as she sprinkled Parmesan cheese over her spaghetti.

"Yeah, why?" Usually when it was Dad's weekend, we'd eat with him on Friday night, but tonight he had to go to dinner with a big radio station advertiser. Mom's hospital shift ended early that day, so she said it was fine to start the weekend with her and that she could take me to the dance.

"Well, he'll be picking you up from the dance."

"That's okay." I didn't know why Mom seemed weirdly nervous about this. We were getting used to the every-other-weekend-at-Dad's-place routine. It wasn't a big deal.

"Okay, good," Mom said. By now she had sprinkled about half a cup of Parmesan onto her plate.

"Mom, what's up with all the cheese?" I asked.

"What?" She looked down and seemed shocked to see how much cheese was there. "Oh geez. Or should I say 'Oh cheese'? Ha!"

I rolled my eyes. "Um, no, you shouldn't say that." Mom was normally not nearly that corny; that was usually Dad's department. "Are you okay?"

She took a deep breath. "Well, I sort of have a date tonight."

I lowered my fork. "What do you mean, 'a date'?"

"A date. A movie with . . . a gentleman. I've been out with him a couple of times before, and I thought you should know."

"Does Dad know?"

"Not yet. I'll tell him eventually. But I'd appreciate it if you keep this between us for now."

"Why did you tell me? I'm not going to be here; I didn't even have to know!"

"Well, it's someone you know, and I thought you should hear it from me instead of from someone else."

"Who is it?" My brain started racing, thinking who I possibly knew who might take our mother out on a date.

Mom took the deepest breath I'd ever seen her take. "It's Charlie Singer."

I was relieved. I had no idea who that was. We didn't know any grown-ups named Charlie. He must be, like, some old college friend of Mom's who I'd met once and she assumed I remembered, but nope.

"Who is that?" I asked. "We don't know any . . ."

And then it hit me.

"Wait. *Singer?* Like *Mr. Singer? My fifth-grade teacher Mr. Singer?* No. Wait. It's not him. Isn't his first name Charles?"

"Yes," Mom said. "But he goes by Charlie. It's a nickname for Charles."

"I KNOW THAT CHARLIE IS A NICKNAME FOR CHARLES! But I can't believe you're dating my teacher!"

"He's not your teacher anymore," Mom said. "He's not a teacher at all anymore." That seemed like an even more ridiculous point.

"Mom, you know what I mean," I said. "It feels like he'll always be my teacher."

"I know, I know," she said. "I realize this must be strange for you. It was strange for me too when it started."

"If it was so strange for you, then why did you go out with him?"

"It kind of just happened, Gus. I ran into him at the Meridian Music Festival over the summer when you girls were at Dad's place. We started talking and decided it would be nice to have dinner together sometime, so we did."

I couldn't believe it. The Meridian Music Festival is in early July. "This started that long ago? And you're just now telling me?"

"A minute ago you were annoyed that I was telling you at all."

"A minute ago I didn't know you were dating my teacher!"

Mom opened her mouth to respond, but I cut her off. "And don't say that he's not my teacher!"

"I wasn't going to say that," Mom said. "I was just going to say that I really do understand why this is weird for you. And that you can talk to me about it whenever you want. But that I hope you'll keep it between us for now."

"I don't want to talk about this with anyone, including you," I said. "So you don't have to worry about that."

Mom looked like she wanted to say more, but just

then we heard a car door close, and you came running in from Clarissa's house.

"Hey, sweet Louie," Mom said, giving your head a rub. "We have to go soon. Gus, you should start getting ready for the dance."

I know it's exciting for a fourth grader to think about a middle-school dance. I know because it had been for me when I was in fourth grade, and because when Mom told me to get ready, your eyes got big and you said, "Ooh, can I watch?!"

But all I was thinking of was Mom, and Mr. Charlie Singer, and getting out of the house as fast as I could without talking to a single soul.

So that's why I ran up the stairs, said a quick "Nope!" and slammed my bedroom door.

# 28. The cackling eighth-grade boys

"What kind of music will there be?"

"Do you get snacks there?"

"Do the teachers go?"

"Who are you going to dance with?"

These were just a few of the questions you asked in the car on the way to the dance, Lou. And I'm pretty sure I said "I don't know, I don't know, I don't know" over and over again. I didn't want to talk about anything. This night was off to a terrible start. Besides the Mr. Singer news, when I went upstairs to change, I couldn't find my favorite black shirt anywhere. The shirt that I'd been planning to wear to the dance. And then I remembered: it was at Dad's. I'd left it there after he took us out for sushi a couple of weeks ago and told me I should be "a little dressy" and not wear my Longwood Art

Camp T-shirt. Yet another way our parents were messing up my life. So now I was stuck wearing a stupid old purple shirt.

Usually I would complain to Mom about this, or even ask if I could borrow something of hers, like her jean jacket to wear over the boring shirt. But I couldn't speak to Mom about my outfit, or anything else. All I could think during the whole ride was *Mom is going out with Mr. Singer. Mom is going out with Mr. Singer. Mom is going out with Mr. Singer.* Up until then, I'd thought the worst news I'd ever hear was that Mom and Dad were getting divorced. But this might just have been worse.

Mr. Singer was one of the first people outside our family who knew about the divorce, other than Layla and a few of Mom and Dad's friends. And I guess you probably told Isabella. We never talked much about it, did we?

Anyway, Mr. Singer didn't hear about the split from me. I didn't want anybody at school other than Layla to know. I figured if I didn't tell anyone, life at school wouldn't have to change the way life at home was changing.

I guess I should've told Mom and Dad that plan. Because, unbeknownst to me, they sent an email to Mr. Singer telling him what was going on. I found out about it when he asked me to talk to him in the hallway one day while the rest of the class was watching a movie about the deepest part of the ocean.

That conversation went something like this:

Mr. Singer: Everything okay, Augusta?

Me: Yes.

Mr. Singer: Anything you need to talk about?

Me: No.

Mr. Singer: *(Pause.)* Okay.

Me: Can I go back inside now?

Mr. Singer: It's just that I got an email from your parents about what's going on at home.

Me: Oh.

Mr. Singer: They said you aren't talking much to them about it. I think they wanted me to sound you out and make sure you're doing all right.

Me: Yup. I'm good. (I desperately, desperately wanted the conversation to be over so I could go back inside and watch the ocean movie and just be a regular kid with no Big Serious Problem that all the adults wanted me to talk about.)

Mr. Singer: Okay. *(Pause again.)* Well, if you think you need to talk, my door is always open.

Me: Okay.

I didn't point out that his door was actually usually closed because our classroom was near the gym and it got noisy. I guess "my door is always open" is just one of those weird expressions that doesn't mean exactly what it sounds like.

Anyway, for the rest of the year, Mr. Singer never tried to get me to talk about anything I didn't want to talk about. He didn't make it into a big deal when I said I'd left my math folder at my dad's apartment and wouldn't be able to get it for a few days. And he certainly didn't act like it was a big tragedy like weirdo Ms. Tedesco did. He was just . . . normal.

But suddenly I was seeing all that differently. That day in the hallway, was he just asking how things were because he wanted to know if Mom was available? When I said I left my folder at Dad's, was he secretly happy to hear they were still living apart? Did he send home love notes to Mom in the sealed envelopes with my report cards? *Ick*.

■ ■ ■

So maybe now you understand why I was so quiet on the way to the dance. I couldn't wait to get away from Mom and leave her to drop you off at Dad's. Which is why I opened the door before the car had even fully rolled to a stop, causing Mom to yell "*Augusta!* You're going to break your neck!" right in front of some eighth-grade boys who were arriving at the same time. And who, of course, started cracking up and screeching "You're going to break your neck, Augusta!" over and over again in high-pitched voices.

I glared at Mom, slammed the car door, and tried to act like everything was normal and cool as I pulled my jacket closed in front of me and walked as quickly as I could past the cackling eighth graders.

*At least the parental-embarrassment part of the evening is over,* I thought as I climbed the steps to the front door.

Turns out I was wrong.

# 29. Laura (and Mary)

It was weird being at school at night. With everyone in the gym, the hallways were darker and quieter, and the floors seemed shinier. I tried to shake off thoughts about Mom and Mr. Singer so I could focus on the plan Sarah and I had discussed:

1. Meet at my locker, which is around the corner from the gym.
2. Put my glasses in my locker so I wouldn't have to wear them into the dance. (Would this make it harder for me to see? Yes, of course. But I had practiced walking around at home and at Dad's apartment without them, and even though everything looked really blurry,

at least I hadn't walked into a wall or fallen down a flight of stairs. I was confident I could handle it. Besides, right then I cared more about how I looked to other people than how they looked to me. Come to think of it, I guess I'd always felt that way.)

3. Walk into the gym.
4. Find a corner where we could sit or stand while we figured out what everyone actually *did* at a middle-school dance.
5. Take it from there.

Right off the bat, things didn't go as I'd hoped. When I got to my locker, Sarah wasn't there, but Davis Davis was.

"Why are you back here?" he asked as soon as he saw me.

"I have to put something in my locker," I said. "Why are *you* back here?" Maybe it was just because we were further into the school year, or maybe it was because I had better and speedier lock skills these days, but I wasn't feeling intimidated by Davis Davis anymore just because he was a year older than me. Also, I think my brief life of crime and punishment had made me tougher.

"None of your business," he said as he lifted a large, drippy can of white paint into his locker.

"It will be my business if that paint leaks from your locker into mine," I said, wondering if it was still safe to hang my jacket in there.

Davis Davis sighed. "If you must know, it's official JROTC business." JROTC stands for Junior Reserve Officers' Training Corps; it's a club where kids practice being in the army, or something like that. Davis Davis takes it very seriously.

"Do you guys have to paint your pretend guns or something?"

He rolled his eyes at me. "They're called *drill purpose rifles*. And *again,* this is for official JROTC business. Not *your* business."

"Fine," I said, leaning against the lockers beside ours.

"Why are you still here?" he asked me.

"I'm meeting someone here! Also, in case you haven't noticed, I'm still waiting to get into my locker."

He rearranged the things in his locker—two more cans of paint, brushes, and something that looked like an old sheet—then slowly and deliberately closed the door. "All yours," he said.

Sarah came running up just as Davis Davis turned to walk away.

"Hey! Sorry I'm late," she said. "My parents had a mix-up about who was supposed to drive me."

I knew how those mix-ups could go. Sarah seemed almost as flustered as I was when I first got here, although I assumed her evening hadn't also included the news that her mom was dating her fifth-grade teacher.

"It's okay. Want to put your jacket in my locker?" Sarah took off her jacket, and I could see she was dressed pretty much the same as I was: black leggings, long T-shirt. This wasn't a surprise since we'd texted back and forth a bunch of times trying to figure out what we should wear. As if it weren't bad enough that this dance had a theme that was insulting to girls and women, we also were encouraged to "dress Dogpatch!" which apparently meant to dress like farmers or cowgirls or something, the way the people in Sadie Hawkins's town had dressed. Which was why the Silver Sisters were planning on matching cowgirl boots. No thank you.

Sarah and I had agreed on the following: no "Dogpatch" gear, no dresses, no skirts. But look a little dressy, which we decided meant no T-shirts with writing on them, and black boots instead of sneakers. Sarah looked great. I was stuck in my old purple shirt, but she was wearing a light blue one that was a little sparkly. And her hair looked wavier than usual. And she was wearing lip gloss. And dangly earrings. I peeked at myself in my locker mirror and suddenly decided that I looked like a mess. Besides the old shirt, my hair looked stringy. A zit was threatening to pop out on my chin. And was there actually something hanging out of my nose?

I found a tissue in my jacket pocket and tried to fix that last one.

"Do you have a hair tie I can borrow?" I asked Sarah. "I feel like I want to pull my hair back. And maybe some lip gloss?"

Sarah dug around in her jacket pockets and found both for me.

"Are you okay?" she asked as she handed me the gloss.

"Yeah," I said. "Just a weird night." I didn't feel like telling anyone the news about Mom and Mr. Singer just yet. Or possibly ever.

"How does this ponytail look?" I asked her after I'd finished pulling my hair back.

"Cute. You look nice!" Sarah was a good friend.

"Not as nice as you. Your hair looks amazing."

"Gah, whatever." She blushed a little as she rolled

her eyes. "My mom convinced me to use her hot rollers; I guess it came out okay."

"Okay, I think I'm ready," I said. I took my glasses off and set them on the top shelf of my locker. My reflection in the mirror was a *little* more reassuring without them (possibly because now it was a bit blurry).

"What do you think?" I asked Sarah.

"Looks great," she said. "So are we going to be like Laura and Mary tonight?"

"Who?"

"You know, Laura and Mary, in the Little House on the Prairie books."

"Yeah . . . but how are we going to be like them?"

"Because after Mary became blind, Laura had to describe everything for her all the time."

"Ha. Yes, will you be my Laura tonight? Describe the land of wonder that is the Meridian Middle School gym, please."

"I'm on it," Sarah said. "Let's do this, Mary."

# 30. DJ Dave

"Huh," Sarah said as we walked through the double doors into the gym. "Laura and Mary would probably feel really at home here, actually."

"What do you mean?" I asked. I could just make out the letters on the big banner across the entryway that said WELCOME TO DOGPATCH! but that was about it. The rest of the room was a blur of cloudy lights and dark figures moving around.

"Well, there's lots of hay," Sarah explained. "And straw hats and cowboy boots."

"Any bonnets?"

"Not yet," Sarah said. "I will let you know the second I see one."

"Please do."

"There are drinks and snacks over there," Sarah said,

pointing to the opposite side of the gym. "Want to get some?"

"Sure," I said. I wasn't particularly hungry or thirsty, but it would give us something to do. I stuck by Sarah's side as we made our way around the edge of the gym to the refreshment stand. Walking directly across the gym would have been faster, but that also would have meant crossing the dance floor. I could see the blurry outlines of a few kids dancing as a DJ switched from one song to another and called out things like "All right, cowpokes! DJ Dave wants to get this party started!" It was somewhat terrifying.

When we got close to the refreshment stand, I could see that it was decorated with a banner made of red bandanas, and the food had labels like CRUNCHY TATERS (potato chips) and TASTY FIXINS (dip and salsa). It seemed like a lot of work, making labels for food that everyone could easily identify anyway. If anything, the labels made it confusing. (This is one reason I was not a member of the dance committee. Unnecessary decorations annoy me.)

My gym teacher, Ms. Lewis, was standing behind the snack table. Her blond ponytail was tied in a red bandana for the occasion. Sarah started to fill a paper bowl with "crunchy taters" when Ms. Lewis leaned toward her in a move that was part reach, part nervous lunge.

"Allow me!" she said, putting a handful of chips in Sarah's bowl. Ms. Lewis eyed Sarah nervously as she moved away from the table with her food. "Watch out for crumbs!" Ms. Lewis said with a smile, but I knew she was dead serious. The dance was clearly threatening to mess with her vision of the perfect gym.

As we moved away from the snacks, I got a closer look at the booth beside the refreshment stand. This one had a banner across two poles that read GET YER PITCHER MADE, and a professional photographer was snapping a picture of a girl and a boy who looked like eighth graders, both dressed in checked shirts, bandanas, and straw hats. The girl was beaming and sitting on the boy's lap, and the boy was sitting on a bale of hay. There was a line of kids trailing along the gym wall, waiting to have their pictures taken. Some of them were coupled off, but there were groups of friends—mostly girls—waiting too. Of course this included the Huggers and the Silver Sisters, who were up next.

Sarah noticed me squinting up at the banner. " 'Get Yer Pitcher Made,' " she read aloud.

"What's with the assumption that people who live in the country don't know how to spell?" she said. "Geez, this dance is all kinds of offensive."

"Why are you guys even here, then?" a voice from the line asked. "I mean, if it's all so offensive."

I looked down from the banner and let my eyes focus on the person who was talking. But I didn't have to. I already knew it was Addison.

Heidi chimed in. "Yeah, a lot of people worked really hard on this dance, you know."

"I'm surprised you guys even came," Addison said. "Are your boyfriends from the courtyard here?"

"Who are you talking about?" I asked at the exact same time Sarah said, "They aren't our boyfriends."

Addison smirked.

"Augusta, you look different," Marcy said. "Did you get contacts?"

"Nah," I said, trying to act like it wasn't a big deal and the entire gym wasn't a big blur to me. "I don't always need to wear my glasses."

"Why didn't you wear them tonight?" Addison asked. "Trying to look different for someone?"

When I shrugged and said I just forgot them, Addison looked at Marcy and said, "You were friends with Augusta in elementary school. Didn't she *always* have to wear glasses then?"

Marcy looked at the floor. "I don't really remember."

"Hmm." Addison moved on. "What about Sarah in elementary school, Heidi? Were you guys friends?"

It was easy to see what Addison was doing. She wanted to make sure Marcy and Heidi knew it was lame that they used to hang out with us (and of course that they'd understand how lucky they were to be friends with her now). Heidi bought into it more than Marcy did.

"*No,*" Heidi said, as though Addison had suggested that she'd eaten a bug. "My mom just made me do ballet carpool with her when we were little."

"True story!" Sarah said. This was different from what Sarah had told me before, which was that she and Heidi had actually been friends for a while. But I wasn't going to bring that up now. "Looks like you guys are up," Sarah said, nodding toward the photographer. It was their turn to get their "pitcher" taken.

"Okay, losers," Addison said to Marcy and Heidi, putting her arms around them and shuffling them toward the photographer. "HEY! LOSERS!" she yelled at Amber and a handful of other girls who were standing nearby, scrolling through their phones. "It's time for our picture!"

They rushed over to join them on a hay bale. How did they know, I wondered, that they were "allowed" to be in the picture with her? As they zipped past me, I noticed they all had matching silver cowgirl boots on; I guess that was the mark of the chosen ones.

"I can't believe she calls her friends losers," I said.

"It's charming, isn't it?" Sarah said. "Let's find a place to sit."

We grabbed cups of lemonade from the refreshment table (where Ms. Lewis still looked anxious about spills) and wandered along the wall until we found an empty hay bale in front of the bleachers.

"So, what's up with you and Marcy?" Sarah asked when we sat down. "Did you guys really used to be friends?"

It was hard to describe what had happened with Marcy; I wasn't sure I understood it myself. But I couldn't blame Sarah for asking. I'd be curious too.

"If I tell you, will you tell me what happened with you and Heidi?" I asked.

Sarah was quiet for a second. "Okay, sure," she said.

"Sooo . . . Marcy and I were friends, but not like best best friends," I said.

"Right," Sarah said. "Layla is your best friend."

I hesitated for a second before repeating, "Right." I hadn't told Sarah that I wasn't really sure where I stood with Layla anymore, now that she was so tight with Jocelyn. One thing at a time.

"Anyway, I was friends with Marcy, but she was kind of annoying. Like, she always had to sit beside me in class and at lunch and on field trips, and sometimes I felt like I couldn't get any space from her."

"Wow, that's hard to imagine now," Sarah said. "No offense."

I laughed a little. "No, I know what you mean. She definitely has gone in a whole other direction this year. She totally changed over the summer, and now she won't even acknowledge that we used to be friends. It's weird." I took a sip of my lemonade. "So . . . what about you and Heidi?"

Sarah sighed. "Well, it was nothing like that. Our moms got to be friends because they'd chat every week in the dance-studio dressing room while Heidi and I were putting our tights and leotards on. Then we started carpooling, and sometimes we'd go to each other's houses after ballet. Heidi was actually kind of nice back then. We used to do art projects and play with her dog. I mean, she definitely always worried about having perfect hair and spotless ballet shoes and being the best dancer and the best artist . . . but I think that was mostly because of her mom. She always put a lot of pressure on Heidi. And she probably still does, which might be why Heidi freaks out about breaking the rules and gets so into stuff like dance decorations, but still wants Addison to think she's cool."

I thought about that for a minute. I almost had to feel bad for Heidi; her mom didn't sound like much fun. And what Sarah told me about her next was even worse.

"Anyway, after a while Heidi's mom started asking me a lot of questions when it was her turn to drive the dance carpool. Mostly about my parents and their divorce, and if they dated other people, and what my grandparents thought, and if it was upsetting for me and Josh. It was weird.

"Then I told my mom about all the questions and she got really annoyed and asked Heidi's mom about it, and it turned into this super-awkward scene in the ballet dressing room one day before a dress rehearsal, about how my mom thought Heidi's mom should mind her own business, and *she* thought my mom should be more sensitive to how I felt about our 'broken home,' and that was pretty much the end of it."

"Wait—she actually said 'broken home'?" I asked.

Sarah laughed. "Yeah. Isn't that crazy? My mom was livid."

I felt like this was as good a time as any to ask my next question. "So, not to be nosy like Heidi's mom, but what did you say when she asked if your parents were dating other people? I mean, were they?"

"I think my dad probably was, but Josh and I didn't know it yet at the time. He has a girlfriend now, but usually he doesn't introduce us to anyone until they've been dating for a long time."

"How many has he introduced you to?"

"This one was the second."

"What about your mom? Does she have a boyfriend?"

"I don't think so." Sarah shook her head. "When me and Josh have our nights with my dad, she usually just hangs out with her sister, my aunt Dina. I don't think she wants a boyfriend."

I wondered if that was true. Why couldn't my mom be more like Sarah's mom, and just be happy to hang out with her sister instead of going on dates with Mr. Singer? (Mom's sister lives in Canada. But still.)

"What's with all the parents-dating questions?" Sarah asked. "What about your mom and dad?"

Now it was my turn to take a deep breath. Just an hour ago, I couldn't have imagined ever telling anyone about Mom and Mr. Singer. Not even Layla. But Sarah talking about her parents and her dad's girlfriends and everything that had gone down with Heidi's mom made me feel better. Safe.

"Well, I don't think my dad has dated anyone," I said. "When it's not our weekend with him, I'm pretty sure he visits my uncle Keith or goes fishing or to concerts with his friends." As the words were coming out of my mouth, though, I wondered. I'd been sure Mom was spending all her free time with her friends Deb and Bonnie, and look how wrong I was about that.

"And your mom?" Sarah asked.

I said it as fast as I could to get it over with. "She's dating my fifth-grade teacher. I just found out tonight. I'm not supposed to tell anyone, so you have to keep it a secret."

"Whoa," Sarah said. "That's some news."

"Tell me about it."

"Did you like your fifth-grade teacher?"

"Yeah," I admitted. "He was my favorite ever. Until now."

"That's a big thing to keep secret," Sarah said. "Why aren't you allowed to tell?"

"I guess she doesn't want my dad to know yet."

"Ugh, I hate that crap," Sarah said. "My parents did the same thing for a long time. 'Don't tell your mother how much these golf clubs cost' or 'Don't tell Dad I let you watch this movie.' Like now that they had us in separate houses, they were allowed to live these crazy secret lives and make us their little spies. It was the worst."

"Do they still do it?"

"Nah. My grandma caught on and told them to cut it out. Also Josh was so stressed he was pulling out his eyebrows, so that made them feel guilty and they eased up."

"Wow." I wondered how I'd look with no eyebrows, and if Mom would break up with Mr. Singer if I pulled them out.

"Good evening, ladies," a voice from above us on the bleachers said. I looked up expecting to see a teacher, but instead it was Syd the tomato kid, calling us "ladies" like someone's dad would do. I should have known it was him.

"Sydney, we're having a conversation," Sarah said.

"I can see that," Syd answered. "What's it about?"

"It's *so* none of your business," Sarah said, giving me a wide-eyed *Can you believe this guy?* look.

Syd was used to this treatment from Sarah. He was undeterred.

"Okay, well, let's talk about something else, then," he said. "Like whether you're going to dance at this dance."

I looked toward the dance floor. It was still blurry, of course, but I could tell that it was definitely more crowded than when we'd first arrived. I suddenly felt nervous: Was Syd actually asking Sarah to dance? Or did he mean both of us? Did he want all of us to dance? Either option seemed too weird to imagine.

"Not likely," Sarah said. She was keeping up the usual cool tone she had with Syd, but I thought her cheeks looked a little pink.

Syd didn't seem to know what to say next either. "Yeah, well, the music sucks anyway," he finally muttered.

He was right about that. It was obvious Heidi was on the dance committee, what with the number of bubble-gummy pop songs and the amount of Spoiler Alert being played. Blech.

I wondered if Nick was there. He would *really* hate this music. Without thinking I wondered it out loud. "Is Nick here?"

Syd's eyes got wide. "Why do you want to know, Gus?" Oh geez. He thought I wanted to dance with Nick. Or something.

"It just made me think of him when you mentioned the music, *Sydney*," I said, giving him my best eye roll.

"Oh, so you were *thinking* of him, huh?" Syd said.

"Geez, cut it out, Sydney," Sarah said, giving his leg a little nudge.

"I'm just messing with you, Gus," Syd said.

I'd noticed that friends of Nick's called me Gus because that was what he called me, even if I hadn't known them before this year. Somehow I didn't really mind it.

"I don't know if he's here. He said he might check the dance out, but I haven't seen him. He also said he expected it to be stupid, and it looks like he wasn't wrong about that."

Why did I feel a little disappointed to hear that Nick wasn't there? Until now, I hadn't given a single thought to whether he would be at the dance or not. I also felt dumb . . . Nick was right: this dance *was* stupid. And I'd known it all along, from the moment Ms. Barakat told us who Sadie Hawkins was, and when I saw how excited people like Heidi were about it. Why had I come?

"What time are you getting picked up?" I asked Sarah.

"Ten."

"What time is it now?"

"Eight-thirty," Syd answered.

Sarah and I groaned at the same time.

"Want to text our parents and see if they can get us sooner?" I asked.

"Let's give it a few more minutes," she said. "Maybe it'll get better." Was it my imagination or did she glance at Syd when she said that?

"Okay, this one's for all you sweethearts out there!" DJ Dave put on Spoiler Alert's cheesiest ballad, and the dance floor cleared in seconds. But a few couples came together like magnets and hugged each other while they swayed to the music.

"Do you guys want to go to the courtyard?" Syd asked.

"Why?" Sarah said. "Are we even allowed?"

Syd shrugged. "It's worth a try. Beats staying here and listening to this awful music."

Sarah looked at me and said, "What do you think?" in a funny way out of the side of her mouth, and I knew she wanted to go. She was a pretty straight shooter when it came to Syd; if she didn't want to go to the courtyard with him, she would have just said so.

"Okay," I said. There was really no reason not to; a few more couples were heading out to the dance floor, and just sitting and watching them felt creepy.

We got as far as the gym doors when we were stopped by Mr. Smeed, who was on chaperone duty and was clearly unhappy about it.

"Halt!" he said, holding his hand out to stop us as we approached the door. "What business do you have in the hallway?"

"Personal business?" Syd said.

It was obvious Syd didn't have Mr. Smeed as a teacher, or he would have known that vague excuses don't fly.

"We're going to the bathroom, Mr. Smeed," I said.

"All three of you?" Mr. Smeed asked, grimacing like he'd caught us in an elaborate lie. "To the *same* bathroom?"

"No," Syd said, playing along with my lie. "I'm going to a different one."

Smeed sniffed. He clearly was disappointed that there wasn't really anywhere to go from there with his interrogation.

"Fine, but make it quick," he said. "Straight to the lavatory and straight back."

It's amazing, the way Smeed still uses words like "halt" and "lavatory." It's like he arrived here in a time machine from . . . I don't know when. Whenever it was that people actually said "halt" and "lavatory."

"Yes, sir!" Syd said, giving Mr. Smeed a salute. Ooh boy, that would never fly in his class either.

"*Go,* Sydney," Sarah murmured, beelining away from Smeed and around the corner to the bathrooms. Luckily, the door to the courtyard is just beyond them.

The air in the courtyard was so cool compared to the swelter of the gym. Walking through that door felt like brushing your teeth after eating a clove of garlic. Even the underlying scent of rotting crab apples was sweeter than the smell in the gym, which seemed to be a combination of sweat, deodorant, and fruity body spray.

"Wow, it seems so different out here at night," Sarah said.

"Yeah," Syd agreed. "Like, even more secret."

There was a rustling sound at the far end of the courtyard, and as my eyes adjusted to the darkness, I saw that we weren't alone. Elaine Farley was already there, kneeling on the grass and collecting crab apples in a plastic bag. I squinted and saw that she was dressed a little nicer than usual, in a gray sweater that was a bit too short for her and boots I'd never seen her wear before.

"What are you guys doing out here?" she asked when she saw us.

"Just wanted some fresh air," Syd said. "Why are *you* out here?"

I wanted him to be careful about how he talked to Elaine. She never talked to me in social-studies class or in the courtyard, but she never talked to *anyone*. I think this was the most I'd ever heard her speak, and it was just one sentence. She was like a wild baby animal, out here alone in the courtyard at night, and I didn't want Syd to scare her.

"No reason," she said.

"Why are you collecting crab apples?" Syd kept pushing. "You know you can't eat those."

"I know. I just thought I'd clean up the courtyard. So we don't have to smell them when we eat lunch."

The way she said *when we eat lunch* made it sound like she actually ate with us every day, and not by herself with a book. I wondered if she noticed that too, because then she said, "I mean, I don't like the smell when I eat anyway."

"So you came here just to clean up crab apples?" Syd said. "Not for the dance?" Syd is a decent-enough guy, and I knew he was genuinely curious and didn't mean to sound like he was grilling her. But that's how it came across.

Elaine looked like she wanted to run away. "No . . . I . . . my parents said I had to . . ."

I tried to think of a way to help her. "You're right," I said. "The apples do smell weird. Do you want us to help you pick them up?"

"I'm not picking—" Syd started to say, but Sarah gave his sneaker a little kick.

Elaine didn't look any less cornered. "I don't have any other plastic bags," she said, gazing down at the one hanging from her fingers.

I was about to say we could all share that one when the courtyard door squeaked open.

"Hey, I thought I might find you guys out here! Do you secretly live here or something?"

The face was blurry, but I'd know that voice anywhere. It was Quincy, flushed and sweaty from dancing in the gym. She let the heavy courtyard door close behind her.

"Why are you all sweaty?" Syd asked.

Quincy gave Syd a look of great pity. "I was dancing," she said. "We're at a dance."

"The music sucks," he said.

"Right—that's why I brought headphones," Quincy said, holding them up to show us. "When the DJ plays a sappy slow song, I put these on and dance to whatever I want. Mekhai was doing it too. It's hilarious. And the dance-committee weirdos hate it."

Quincy is something else. She literally dances to the beat of a different drummer.

"Anyway, I wanted to tell you Smeed is looking for you. He had kids check the bathrooms and he knows you aren't there."

Before that information could even sink in, the courtyard door opened again, this time with a bang against the brick wall. Of course it was Mr. Smeed.

# 31. DJ Z

"I might have known this group would be doing something illicit," Smeed said, shining his phone flashlight in our faces.

"Wow, *illicit*," Quincy muttered. "That sounds super serious." Sarah stifled a giggle.

"Back into the gym. NOW!" Smeed yelled. "There will be no more 'trips to the bathroom' for any of you." He made air quotes with his fingers as he said it. "You're staying in the gym."

Suddenly even the air in the courtyard felt stifling, and my plan to text Dad for early pickup seemed like a lifeline. "I might need to go home early," I said.

Smeed glared at me. "There is no *going home early*, Miss Reynolds. This event ends at ten, and you five are here until the bitter end. Now get back in that gym unless you want me to take this matter to Mr. Wyatt."

As we shuffled back to the gym, Syd asked, "Is that legal? To say we can't leave? They can't hold us here against our will, can they?"

"No," Quincy said. "They can't. But I bet if any of us text our parents and try to get out early, Smeed will go straight to Wyatt and say we were in the courtyard when we weren't supposed to be."

"Yeah, and you guys would be repeat offenders after your homeroom gambling ring," Syd said.

I gave him a look. "Thanks for reminding us."

"You're welcome!" Syd grinned, and Sarah gave him another little kick. At this rate he'd have a hole in his sneaker by the end of the night.

Back in the gym, not much had changed. If the song that was playing wasn't by Spoiler Alert, it was by someone who sounded exactly like them. I was starting to get a headache, probably from a combination of the crappy music and the fact that I hadn't seen anything clearly all night.

Elaine Farley had thrown her bag of crab apples away and was now sitting on a hay bale. I was debating whether to sit down beside her when a new voice came over the speakers.

"Hey, Meridian . . . get ready to have your minds blown." And then the music changed. Like, *really* changed. The sound coming out of the speakers was a staccato guitar that was somehow happy and dark at the same time. I recognized it in a split second. It was the sound of my very favorite dance song, "Blister in the Sun," and I couldn't believe DJ Dave would play it.

Turns out, he wouldn't.

Standing at the DJ table, his head barely clearing the microphone stand, was none other than Nick Zambrano. He raised both arms and shouted, "I'm DJ Z!"

"Whoa, it's Zambrano!" Syd looked happier than he had all night. It's possible that I did too. Good music makes a big difference.

"Hey, DJ Z," Syd yelled toward the DJ stand. "What are you doing there?"

Nick waved us over. I noticed Amber watching as we crossed the gym toward him. She turned back to the other Silver Sisters when I caught her eye.

"I've been back and forth between here and the snack table all night." Nick was talking faster than usual. "I told DJ Dave I know how to use all his equipment. He didn't believe me, but he let me play one song while he watched. He picked the song, though.

"Then I started bringing him a ton of water so he'd

have to leave his post and go to the bathroom. I hoped maybe he'd let me cover for him. And it worked!"

Nick took a deep breath. "Didn't you guys see me over here?"

"I thought I might have at one point," Syd said. "But I've been kind of distracted." He glanced at Sarah out of the corner of his eye. Her cheeks looked pink again.

"I didn't see you," I said. "But I can't really see anything."

Nick looked at me for a long second. "Oh yeah, where are your glasses?"

"I forgot them at home," I lied.

"Well, now you can dance like crazy without worrying about them flying off!" he said.

"Ha, yeah, right."

"No, I'm serious. I figure we only have till the end of this song before DJ Dave comes back and shuts me down. Lucky for us it's a good one."

"I'll just listen," I said.

"Come on, Gus," Nick said. "I remember you and Louie doing routines to this in your backyard. You know how to dance to this one. Even I do."

He stepped out from behind the DJ booth and held his hand out to me. And for a second, I thought about taking it. I did. Dancing to "Blister in the Sun" would definitely have been the most fun thing to happen that night, even if it was with goofy Nick Zambrano.

But then a bunch of other things happened at once.

Heidi must have seen Nick reaching for my hand, because I saw her nudge Amber, whose mouth dropped open when she looked over at us.

DJ Dave appeared in the doorway and started walking quickly and purposefully back to his booth.

And then, out of nowhere, I felt a sharp, bruising pinch to my backside.

"Ha, I gotcha, Four Eyes!" the Gooser cackled as he pivoted around to face me.

I felt tears spring up in my eyes, and I tried to will them not to spill out onto my cheeks. I looked up at his doughy, greasy face and couldn't think of a thing to say. But I forced myself to meet his eyes.

"Didn't think I'd recognize you without your glasses, did you?" he said. "I'd know that butt anywhere."

One tear spilled out. The rest threatened to follow.

"Hey! What's wrong with you, man?" Nick's face was as red as mine felt.

"Who are you, her boyfriend?" The Gooser bent down to put his face inches from Nick's.

"You're a jerk," Nick spat at him. "Get away from us."

The Gooser looked like he was going to say more,

but at that moment DJ Dave yelled over from where he'd been standing at his sound board, presumably deleting any songs Nick had cued up.

"Hey, *DJ Z*!" he hollered. "Next time you offer to man my station, stay there. Don't take off to see your girl."

Of course this brought another cackle from the Gooser. "Ha, I told you! Four Eyes has a boyfriend."

How did this guy get away with being so awful? He finally turned to leave, probably looking for another butt to pinch. But this time he didn't get very far. In fact, he fell down. Rather spectacularly, actually. In the pause between songs, everyone on that side of Dogpatch had the pleasure of hearing sweaty, doughy Gooser face meet hard gym floor.

As he scrambled to get to his feet, I saw Elaine Farley quickly pull her foot back and turn away on her hay bale.

The Gooser was enraged. "Who did that? What happened?" His head swiveled around as he tried to figure out who or what had tripped him. His eyes never even stopped on Elaine. It was like she was invisible to him.

"Dude, your nose is bleeding." Syd pointed up at the Gooser's face and grimaced.

The Gooser put his hand up to his nose, cursed, and

ran out of the gym. Other girls' bottoms would be safe for the rest of the night. But mine was still hurting. My song was over. Amber was glaring at me. I wanted to go home.

"You okay, Gus?" Nick asked.

"Yeah," I lied again. "I'm just ready for this to be over."

But it wasn't over yet. Now that DJ Dave was back in charge, there were more Spoiler Alert songs to suffer through. Sarah and I hit the refreshment table again. Nick and Syd followed close behind. They started throwing popcorn at each other and trying to catch it with their mouths, until Ms. Lewis spied them and put a stop to it.

After what felt like an eternity, DJ Dave finally announced it was the last song of the night, and he replayed the cheesy Spoiler Alert ballad. All the couples from before—and a few new ones—moved out to the dance floor.

"Smeed's letting kids out now," Sarah said. "Let's go get our stuff."

If Smeed noticed Sarah and me filing out with other kids on our way to the lockers, he didn't say anything. Nick wasn't so lucky, though.

"Mr. Zambrano." Smeed clapped a hand on Nick's

shoulder and stopped him from following us out the door. "We need some help stacking these hay bales."

Nick looked at Smeed like he was crazy, but I knew he didn't dare argue. Our entire homeroom was on thin ice after the Binaca incident. I stepped up my pace before Smeed could turn and ask me too.

For once, Davis Davis wasn't blocking my locker, so I got my jacket and my glasses quickly and met up with Sarah outside. We were standing by the flagpole when a stampede of silver boots approached us.

"I thought you forgot your glasses," Addison said.

"Yeah," Heidi chimed in. "We figured maybe that's why you were dancing with Nick even though you know Amber likes him. Because surely you must have thought he was someone else since you're blind."

"*Heidi,*" Amber hissed. Addison rolled her eyes and said, "Come *on,* Amber." I actually agreed with her; it was ridiculous for Amber to pretend that her crush on Nick was a secret anymore.

"She wasn't dancing with him," Sarah said. "We were all just talking."

"Gus!" It was Nick, coming through the front doors and waving at me. How had he gotten out of hay-bale duty so quickly?

He jogged down to where Sarah and I were standing.

"Smeed had to let me go because my mom texted that she was here. Do you need a ride?"

I couldn't bear to look at anyone at that moment— not Nick, not Sarah, and certainly not the Silver Sisters. But I didn't have to look at them. I could feel Amber's glare like the sun on my skin.

I started to say I was going to my dad's, so it would be out of the way for Nick's mom anyway. But before I could say anything, Addison's voice cut through my thoughts.

"What. Is. That."

I turned in the direction she was looking, and then I saw it. The perfectly horrible end to a perfectly horrible night. It was you, Lou, and Dad, rolling up to the curb in the giant green-and-orange WOLD van. Why? Why? God, why?

# 32. Officer Baldwin

"Is that your *car*?" Heidi shrieked.

"No," I answered.

"Well, isn't that your dad?" Addison said. "What'd he do, steal it?" She, Amber, and Heidi were practically in tears, they were laughing so hard. Marcy knew where my dad worked. She just smiled and examined her bangle bracelets.

"It's his work car," Nick said, as though I couldn't speak for myself. "He works at the radio station." He raised his hand and waved. "Hey, Mr. Reynolds!"

You might remember the rest, Lou. Because that's when I quickly said "bye" to Sarah and bolted to the van. You waved goodbye to Nick. I didn't.

I couldn't believe Dad had picked me up from my first dance in the stupid WOLD van. I couldn't believe

the kids at school—including the horrid Silver Sisters—
had seen it. I couldn't believe I was having to ride home
wedged between sound equipment in the back. I could
barely even listen as Dad apologized about the van and
tried to explain about his car not starting again, and
how his boss had given him a ride to the station after
their client dinner and said he could use the van. I just
wanted to be home. And not Dad's apartment either—
*home* home, where we'd lived our whole lives and where
Mom still was. And then I remembered: No, Mom was
not at home right now. Mom was on a date. With Mr.
Singer. UGH.

But I couldn't even say anything about it. Because it
was a big secret from you and Dad.

And that's when I heard the siren, and saw the flash-
ing lights. That's when Dad looked in the rearview mirror, said "What the heck?" and pulled over. And then
a tall policeman walked up to the car and introduced
himself as Officer Baldwin.

Turns out you and Dad would find out about Mom
and Mr. Singer soon enough.

# 33. Officer Perry

The next morning, I got that terrible feeling you get when you wake up and for a second you think it's a normal day, but then you remember all the things that went horribly wrong the night before. Like all the bad music at the dance. And the hostile looks from the Silver Sisters. And being pinched by the Gooser. And getting picked up in the WOLD van in front of half the school. And, just when it seemed like things couldn't get any worse, winding up at a police station late at night with you, Dad, Officer Baldwin, Mom, and Mr. Singer.

Mr. Singer seemed to be in a pretty good mood, even though his date was being interrupted. Maybe he knew he had to put on a good face in a ridiculously awkward situation. Mom didn't look quite so pleased. I thought she listened pretty calmly as Dad explained how we'd been pulled over because the WOLD van had a broken taillight. But you and I both knew that mood was going to go south quickly when she heard the rest of the story. About how Officer Baldwin next noticed that Dad wasn't wearing a seat belt. Because the driver's-side seat belt was broken.

Mom didn't seem to care much about Dad's explanation: that he hadn't worried about the broken seat belt because he was so flustered about his car not starting and having to borrow the WOLD van in the first place. And that that was why she and Mr. Singer had to interrupt their date to come to the police station, because Officer Baldwin declared the van was unsound for driving, and said we'd have to go to the station with him and find another way home.

So the main thing I was remembering the next morning was the yelling. The "How could you drive our children in a car with a broken taillight *and* a broken seat belt, Matt—how could you not notice those things?" from Mom and the "I don't know, Shelly; apparently there's a lot I haven't noticed!" from Dad as he glanced at Mr. Singer.

I think that was when Officer Perry came in and offered to show us the vending machine. I knew she was just trying to get us away from an awful scene between our parents, but I went along with her even though I wasn't hungry. I couldn't believe you bought and ate a whole bag of chips, Lou, but then you never seem to get stressed out.

Remember? I even asked you about it.

"Doesn't this bother you at all?"

"What?" you said, munching on a chip.

"The fact that we're in a police station and Dad is in trouble and Mom is here with Mr. Singer?"

"Oh," you answered. "Well, we got to ride in a police car. That was cool. And Mr. Singer is nice. Can you hold my chips? I have to go to the bathroom."

ARGH.

While Officer Perry walked you to the bathroom, I couldn't stop thinking about how awful it was to have to see Mr. Singer in that situation. How I'd tried to stop Dad from calling Mom when we needed a ride, but how he insisted that she was going to have to know sooner or later (and also Uncle Keith was in Florida, so he couldn't pick us up). How I'd hoped that she'd have the good sense to at least leave Mr. Singer and get us by herself, and how sick I felt when I could tell that she was explaining to Dad over the phone that her date would be coming with her, and that her date was Mr. Singer.

Before you came back from the bathroom, Mr. Singer

found me and said, "I know this must be weird for you, Augusta; I hope you're doing okay." And I just looked at him instead of saying what I wanted to say, which was "If you really wanted me to be okay, you wouldn't be dating my mom." That was when you and Officer Perry came back, so he didn't have a chance to say more. Thankfully.

···

So, yeah, that all came flooding back into my brain when I woke up the morning after the dance. I pulled my covers over my head and decided I was going to spend the day like that when I remembered something else: *Ama.* I wasn't even halfway to the amount of money I needed for contact lenses. I had to go to work.

# 34. Scooter

I reached for my phone, which was charging on my bedside table. With everything that had gone down the night before, Dad had forgotten about our family no-phone-in-the-bedroom-overnight rule.

I had a text from Layla: *How was ur dance?!*

Ugh. The last thing I was in the mood for was talking about the dance with Layla. She'd texted me some pictures of her first dance at Parkwood last weekend, and of course it was perfect. The DJ played the best music! The panther mascot was there and he did the limbo! She and her friends were dancing with cute boys! Of course Jocelyn was in the pictures, right there at the center of the awesomeness.

I didn't respond to Layla's text.

I did respond to a text from Sarah that said, *How ru doing today?*

*2 much 2 tell right now*

*Going to Ama's*

*Text u later*

It was weird. A few months ago, I barely even knew Sarah, and now I was dying to talk to her, but I couldn't bring myself to respond to Layla at all. And I'd known her almost my whole life. Sometimes it felt like she was on another planet, instead of just in a different school.

**. . .**

"Gusta! You have to come upstairs!" Ama called from the top of the steps when I walked in. (Her dad had dropped me off in their driveway and left to do errands. He had given me a ride since *my* dad was suddenly without transportation.) "You have to come now!"

I love the way Ama says my name. It's like a combination of the two names everyone else calls me, Augusta and Gus, and in her little voice it is so cute.

"Okay, let me take off my shoes," I called up to her. Dr. Chen isn't strict about many rules in their house, but one thing she takes super seriously is the no-shoes-past-the-foyer rule. Mom says it makes sense because you don't want people tracking dirt into your house when you have a baby. It isn't a big deal except on the days that Ama wants to keep running back and forth from inside the house to the backyard; then I practically have to tackle her to make sure she doesn't either run inside in her sneakers or outside in her socks.

Dr. Chen popped her head around the kitchen doorway. She was holding baby George and her hair was in a messy ponytail.

"Hey, Augusta," she said. She smiled, but her voice sounded tired. "You can go ahead up and hang with Ama. I don't know if you can tell, but she's dying to see you. I think she wants to introduce you to someone. And then, if you don't mind, I might nap with George. We're both pooped."

"Oh, okay," I said. "We'll try to keep quiet."

"Thanks, Augusta." Dr. Chen's shoulders relaxed as she switched George to her other arm and carried him toward her bedroom. I looked at his sleepy little face and thought how sweet and easy life must be when you're a baby. Lucky George.

"*Gusta!*" Ama was really beginning to lose her cool now that I'd been there a whole three minutes and still hadn't made it upstairs. "*I need you!*"

"Okay, I'm coming!" I said in a loud whisper. "But

we have to be quiet so we don't wake Mama and George."

That was obviously of little concern to Ama. She ignored her mother's pat on the head as she walked by, and as I made my way up the stairs she started jumping and clapping her hands. When I got to the top of the stairs, she grabbed me by the wrist and pulled me toward her room.

"Okay, look!" she said as we walked through her doorway. She gestured toward a little table set with plates, teacups, a teapot, and a vase of fake flowers. Around the table were four empty chairs.

"It's a tea party!" she squealed, blatantly ignoring the quiet rule.

"Ooh, it sure is!" I said. "Who are you inviting to it?"

"You! And me! And also my two other friends!"

"Your two other friends? When are they coming?" I was wondering how I was going to handle three kids here and keep them quiet while Dr. Chen napped.

"They're already here!" Ama said, like she couldn't believe I hadn't seen them. "This is Scooter," she said, gesturing toward one of the empty chairs.

"Scooter?" I was about to ask Ama who Scooter was when she made another introduction.

# 35. Granola

"And this is Granola," she explained, pointing to another empty chair.

"Oh, okay," I said, realizing I was in the presence of Ama's imaginary friends (and relieved that no more actual four-year-olds were coming over). "I can't believe I didn't notice them."

"You sit here," Ama said, pointing to the chair beside Granola.

I took a seat and leaned over to Granola's spot. "Granola, it's so nice to meet you," I said. "You must be nice if you're a friend of Ama's."

"No, Granola's not nice," Ama said, shaking her head. "She does the wrong thing sometimes."

"Well, everyone does the wrong thing *some*times," I said. "What kinds of things does Granola do?"

"She plays with Mommy's phone when she's not supposed to. And once she was so noisy that she woke baby George."

"Hmm. Did you talk to her about that?"

"Yes," Ama sighed. "But she's still naughty."

"What about you, Scooter?" I asked, turning toward the other chair. "Are you naughty too?"

"Scooter won't talk to you," Ama said. "She only likes to talk to me. She only wants to be *my* friend."

I was running out of ideas. "Should we just have tea, then?" I suggested.

That was the moment Ama was waiting for. She was out of the room in a flash, running to the bathroom to fill the teapot with water.

And for the second time that day, I felt envious of one of the Chen kids. What if real friends could be like imaginary friends, and you could make them do whatever you wanted? What if I could say to Jocelyn, "No, Layla only wants to be friends with *me*!" and it actually worked? And what if I had another friend like Granola, who would take the fall for me whenever I did something wrong? Is that how I would know when I had my village? My "people" that Ms. Barakat talked about?

That seemed too easy. I doubted I'd ever feel as sure about my people as Ama did about hers.

# 36. Finley

When Ama's dad took me back to Dad's apartment that
night, you guys were busy setting up the new fish tank
you'd bought at the pet store around the corner from
Dad's place while I was out. Dad said we could go back
to the store the next morning if I wanted to pick out
another fish or decorations for the tank, but I told him
what you guys got was fine. I think he was worried that
I'd be mad about not having been included on the fish-
shopping trip, but I didn't care. That kind of thing bothers you more than it bothers me, Lou. I'm more bothered
by things like, say, our mother dating my teacher.

Dad must have known that was on my mind, because he called me into the kitchen with him while you
were setting up the hot-pink gravel in the aquarium.
Finley, the fish you'd named, was swimming around

in Grandma Dotty's big glass pitcher as she waited for her new home to be ready. It was weird being at Dad's apartment and seeing something that once lived in our house with Mom. Especially something Mom had used all the time; she had made so much lemonade in that pitcher. But when Dad moved out she said he should take it with him since Grandma Dotty was his mother. So here it was, looking extra bright and cheery in Dad's mostly beige kitchen, like it was trying to convince itself, and us, that we all belonged here. Finley looked confused; I wonder if she felt as out of place in her new home as the rest of us did.

"Do you want to talk about last night at all?" Dad asked once we were in the kitchen. "With everything else that went on, I didn't even get to hear how the dance was."

"I don't want to talk about the dance," I said.

Dad looked at me for a second, then started putting cups in the dishwasher. "Okay," he said. "Do you want to talk about anything else? Like Mom and Mr. Singer?"

"I'm sorry I didn't tell you," I said. "I only found out right before the dance." I didn't want to tell Dad that Mom had specifically asked me not to tell him. I didn't want to give them another reason to fight.

"I don't care about that, Gus. Besides, it's not your

job to tell me. I just wonder if you want to talk about it at all. With me . . . or we can call Mom if you want. I know it must be kind of weird for you."

"Yeah. I don't really know what to say about it. Can I just help with the fish tank?"

"Okay," Dad said. He didn't really know what else to say either.

That's when I went out to the living room and saw you doing something strange: you were putting some of the gravel into a little ziplock bag. When I asked what you were doing, you said, "I just need it," then turned almost as pink as the gravel and ran with it back to our room. I figured you were squirreling it away to use in another one of your goofy potions.

I wondered if you were thinking at all about Mom and Mr. Singer, or about Dad and his crummy car luck, or me and what had happened at the dance. I thought about how you always seemed to be thinking about little things like potions and aquarium gravel and trading stickers with Isabella when there were much bigger things going on.

But now I know I was wrong about you, Lou. I'm sorry.

# 37. The Gooser's neighbor

Dismal as the dance had been on Friday night, I was still glad to be going back to school Monday morning. Sunday night at home was just too weird. I hadn't wanted to go back to Mom's house at all, but we had to since Dad still had no car. He was going to pick it up from the shop Monday morning, and there wouldn't be enough time to do that and get us off to school on schedule. So back to Mom's we went. Apart from the world's most awkward gathering in the police station, that was the first time Mom was seeing me since the dance. And when she asked how it went, I said, "It was fine, whatever," like I usually did when you guys asked me about anything related to middle school. How can you explain how weird and uniquely unfun a middle-school dance is to a fourth grader? Or to your mother? Even if I wasn't still upset with her for the business with Mr. Singer. Which I was. No thank you. That's why I told you guys I wasn't feeling great and spent the night texting Sarah in my room.

Lou, that was the night—well, one of the nights—when you came into my room and asked if I wanted to play Garbage, the card game you learned at after-school. And I yelled at you not to come in without knocking. And even after you went back out into the hallway and knocked, I still yelled that no, I didn't want to play cards, and said I needed space. And *you* yelled that I never play with you anymore, and I always need space. Which I know is kind of true. And maybe not much fun for you.

■■■

Sarah was waiting by the flagpole when I got to school. I started to put my backpack on the low wall that ran around the flag area when a familiar voice yelled, "Watch it!" It was Davis Davis. He and some of his JROTC buddies were giving the dingy wall a new coat of white paint. I guess he'd had a solid plan for the paint in his locker after all. I noticed that Tyler Peterson was helping him. Even though Tyler was a wing nut, I guess I was glad for him that he was making friends who weren't the Beatles.

"You can't put your backpack there!" Davis said. "JROTC painting project."

"This part hasn't been painted yet," I told him.

"Doesn't matter. This area is restricted until the project is completed."

"Okay, okay," I said, hoisting my bag back up onto my shoulder and rolling my eyes. What was Davis Davis going to be like as a grown-up if he was this serious now?

"How was this morning with your mom?" Sarah asked as we started walking around back to the sixth-grade doors and away from the JROTC painters. She knew I was barely speaking to Mom last night.

"Ugh, I don't know. She had an early shift at the hospital, so I didn't see her much, luckily."

Sarah nodded. "This one could be awkward for a while, huh? What if Mr. Singer becomes your stepdad?"

Like I hadn't already thought of that supremely insane scenario. "Ew, Sarah, you don't have to say that out loud!" I said, chucking my hip into hers. She laughed. I couldn't imagine talking like this with Layla about the Mom–Mr. Singer situation. Her family was too perfect.

Knowing that Sarah had also been through weird stuff with her parents made it easier to joke with her about mine.

"Meet you in the courtyard?" Sarah said as we went our separate ways for homeroom.

"Yerp." Even though it was November, the weather was decent enough for courtyard lunch, and I was glad. I didn't want to have to face the Silver Sisters in the cafeteria today.

There was one person I did want to see, though, and it was someone I normally didn't talk to. Elaine. As I sat through homeroom and then science, I thought about what I wanted to say to her. When I got to social studies, she was already there, quietly huddled over a book at her desk, as usual.

I slid into the seat behind hers, which was still empty. "Hey, Elaine," I said, leaning forward and tapping her shoulder. "I wanted to thank you."

She turned and looked around, like she was unconvinced I was actually talking to her.

"Thank me for what?" she asked. She seemed suspicious, like this might be a joke.

"For Friday," I said. "For tripping the Gooser. That was amazing."

"What's the Gooser?" she asked.

I couldn't believe she didn't know him by his nick-name. I thought the whole school knew. I actually had to think for a few seconds before I remembered his real name.

"Ronald Gosley," I said. "The Gooser. You tripped him after he pinched me at the dance."

Elaine's cheeks turned a bit red. "Oh yeah," she said. "He's my neighbor. He's been doing that to girls since we were little. I'm sick of it."

"Me too!" I said. "I can't imagine having that jerk for a neighbor! Does he ever get in trouble for it?"

"Not really," she said. "My parents always just said, 'Some boys are like that, so just stay away from him.'"

"That's not fair," I said. "Why should you have to change what you do when he's the one who's wrong?"

"Yeah, I guess," she said. "Did you tell your parents about the pinching?"

"No, not yet."

"Why not?"

"Well . . . they've kind of had a lot going on lately. Besides, if no one else here is telling any adults about it, I guess I don't want to be the one tattletale baby who can't handle it."

"I know what you mean," Elaine said. Her face

changed slightly. She looked nervous now, more like her usual self. "You didn't tell anyone I tripped him, did you?"

"No," I said. "But it was awesome; you should be proud!"

"I still have to live near him," she said. "Please just don't tell anyone."

"Okay," I said. "It'll be our secret."

Elaine was about to turn back around when I had another thought.

"Hey, are you eating lunch in the courtyard today?" I asked.

"I always do," she said. "Even when it's cold and you guys aren't there."

"Oh. Well, do you want to sit with me and Sarah today?"

Again, the suspicious face for a couple of seconds. But then she nodded.

"Yeah, okay," she said.

"Cool." It felt like the least I could do after what Elaine did to the Gooser.

# 38. The graffiti

"Okay, so I'll see you in the courtyard?" Elaine asked when the bell rang to release us from social studies and Ms. Tedesco. She phrased it as a question, like she wondered if I'd changed my mind about asking her to eat with us.

"Sure," I said. "I just need to stop by my locker first." I did still want Elaine to sit with us in the courtyard, but now I was wondering if it had been a bad idea to ask her before checking with Sarah. It wasn't as though Sarah would say Elaine couldn't eat with us—she wasn't like Addison and Heidi—but, well, Elaine wasn't exactly the easiest person to talk to. And she didn't know about our parents, or how we felt about the Silver Sisters, or my contact-lens fund—could we really cover any of those things with her there?

Maybe if I hurried, I could get to the courtyard before Elaine and give Sarah a heads-up. Let her know that Elaine was really okay, and that I felt like inviting her to eat with us was the right thing to do after she tripped the Gooser on Friday.

But as usual, one person was going to make it impossible for me to get anywhere fast. Davis Davis. When I got to my locker, he was already there, drying paintbrushes on a rag with military precision and meticulously wrapping them in paper towels before putting them in his locker.

"Can I just put my backpack away real quick?" I asked.

"I don't know—can you?" He gave me a glance as he slowly reached down to pick up another freshly rinsed paintbrush.

"*Davis*. It will take me two seconds. You're going to be here forever."

"I got here first. You can wait."

"*Ugh,* forget it." With my backpack still full of books, I turned to zip down the hall toward the courtyard. As I rounded the corner, I saw right away that I hadn't beaten Elaine there. Or Sarah. Or Nick. In fact, I hadn't beaten *anyone* there, and there were even more kids than usual crowded around the courtyard door, trying to see something. Some were quiet; others were nudging their friends, pointing, and laughing.

"What are you guys looking at?" I tried to peer in between Sarah and Elaine, who were actually standing right next to each other. Nick, who was beside them with Syd, pointed. "You might need to get higher," he said in a low voice.

I stood on tiptoe to get a better look. And then I saw what the other kids were seeing. On the far wall of the courtyard, near where Elaine sat every day with her book, was kind of a rough mural. Stick figures with big heads and exaggerated features. One girl with tangled hair. Another with a serious frown. A third with giant glasses. Boys too: One who had ratty-looking hair and a dopey smile. One with spotty freckles on a goofy-looking face. It almost looked like something Ama would draw. But Ama would never have written the names under the figures: Elaine, Sarah, Augusta, Nick, Syd. No, Ama would never have done something so immature, or so mean.

I sank back down off my tiptoes. I didn't need to keep looking.

"Do you guys want to get out of here?" Nick was looking at me, Sarah, Elaine, and Syd.

I nodded, and Sarah and Syd said "Yeah" at the same

time. Elaine looked stunned; I hoped she knew she could come with us.

"Maybe we can hang in the stairwell," Nick said. I figured he was thinking the same thing I was thinking, that he didn't want to go to the cafeteria now more than ever.

We were about ten steps down the hall toward the stairwell when I felt a hand on my shoulder and heard a voice saying "Not so fast," like I was a villain in a cartoon. I knew right away who that meaty hand and ridiculous cartoon voice belonged to. Smeed.

"You five. Where are you going? The cafeteria's the other way."

"We have to go—" Nick started to say.

"You have to go where?" Smeed snapped. "Far away from the scene of your crime?"

"*Our* crime?" Sarah said. "What do you mean?"

"You were in the courtyard on Friday night during the dance. When I made you return to the gym, I should have investigated out there to see what you were up to. Especially knowing what Mr. Zambrano and Ms. Reynolds are capable of."

"*I* wasn't in the courtyard!" Nick protested. "I was DJ'ing."

"How do I know you didn't slip in later to add to

your friends' drawings?" Smeed said. "Besides, your name is right there on the wall with theirs. You signed your work!"

Nick looked stunned. "Why would any of us paint stupid pictures of ourselves?" he said. "That doesn't make any sense."

"Sense is something you don't seem to have a lot of, Mr. Zambrano. Maybe detention would knock some into you."

"*Detention?*" Nick's tone said what we were all thinking. "For something we didn't do?"

"Wait, how come they got silent lunch before, but this gets detention?" Sarah asked.

"Vandalism and destruction of school property are very serious offenses," Smeed said, barely able to contain his glee as he rattled off those accusations. "And that is exactly what I will tell your parents when I call them. Now come with me to the main office."

The hot tears I felt building in my eyes stung even more than the ones I'd had when I took the thirteen sprays of Binaca. Turns out the only thing worse than getting in trouble for something you did is getting in trouble for something you didn't do.

# 39. Mad Music Mom

"I . . . cannot . . . believe"—the muscles in Mom's face looked like they were made of steel—"that this is the second time this year that I have been interrupted at work with a phone call from Mr. Wyatt saying that my *sixth grader* is involved in *criminal activity at school.*"

"Mom, I swear I didn't do it!" I said as I closed the car door behind me and tossed my backpack into the back seat.

"Never mind. This is not something we are even going to talk about now." Her words were coming out in angry spurts. She wasn't using contractions. "We are going to wait until we are home with your father. In fact, we will not talk at all during this car ride. We will listen to music."

Mom lunged for the power button when she saw me

start to reach toward the car radio. "*My* music!" she yelled. It was useless. I looked out the car window.

Mom started jamming her finger at the preset buttons on the car radio, probably looking for a song that matched her anger. When she finally found one—it was called "Welcome to the Jungle"—she turned it up almost as loud as it would go and drummed fiercely on the steering wheel. If I had made the music that loud, she would have yelled at me to turn it down right away. But I knew better than to yell at that moment. I put up my hood to try to block out some of the sound. It didn't work.

When we got home, Dad was there waiting. I saw that he had his car back, and wondered how much the repairs had cost. Another expense they'd use as an excuse to postpone buying contacts, no doubt. At least I finally had some money of my own.

"Well, Augusta, what do you have to say for yourself?" Dad said as soon as I was in the door, kicking off my shoes. "Moreover, can you tell me what I should say to my boss, since I keep having to leave work for your antics?"

"You didn't have to leave work," I said. "But it's pretty funny that the only time you guys see each other is when I'm in trouble at school. Oh, or when you're in trouble with the police, Dad."

"I don't think that's funny AT ALL, Augusta." Dad's face was starting to get as red as Mom's did in the car. "And I hope you've been saving your money from the Chens, because it's all going to pay for supplies to clean up that school courtyard."

"Are you kidding me?" I said. "That's my contact-lens money. I didn't do anything!"

But Mom was quieter now. "Wait. Is that what's going on here, Gus?" she said. "Do you keep getting into trouble so you can get Dad and me together again?"

Oh boy. "*No,* Mom," I said. "I'm not a little kid. I know that's not how that stuff works. Besides, now everyone knows you wanted to be divorced, so that would just be weird. And, like, fake."

Mom's voice got even quieter. "Okay. Well, does this last problem at school have something to do with Mr. Singer?"

"You aren't listening to me! I. DIDN'T. DO. ANY-THING. Not this time. Yes, it's weird that you're dating Mr. Singer. It's also weird that even though you and Dad get along most of the time, you still don't talk to each other about things like broken seat belts, and whether or not one of you is dating my teacher! You have to tell each other that stuff. It can't be up to me and Louie. It's not fair."

Mom's face turned pink. She looked down at the floor, and then glanced at Dad out of the corner of her eye.

"But whatever," I said, suddenly wishing I hadn't gotten so serious about family stuff. "What I'm saying is, this has nothing to do with all that. I don't know who painted the wall, but Mr. Smeed hates me and Nick, and he just wants to think the worst of us no matter what. But you know me better than he does. Does that really seem like something I'd do?"

Dad sighed. "No, Gus, it doesn't. But neither did the Binaca bet, and you owned up to that. Sometimes this year we feel like we *don't* really know you that well anymore."

"Yeah, well, there's a lot of that going around," I said, glancing at Mom. "I don't know what to say to you guys anymore. Believe what you want."

As I headed upstairs, I was waiting for them to make me come back and get my punishment. But neither of them said anything. I didn't hear them talking until after I was in my room with my door closed, and then it was much quieter than before.

# 40. Your sister

I had to listen to my own loud rage music now, but I
didn't want Mom and Dad to hear it. I just needed to
disappear into the sound and let it drown out everything
else in my head.

My headphones weren't hanging in their usual spot
over my closet door. I had a pretty good idea they'd
been "borrowed" by a certain sister (yes, you, Lou), and
that's when I went into your room to look for them.

I figured it wouldn't take long to find them since your
room is always so organized (unlike mine). The messiest
thing in there was Iris, rubbing her doggy back on your
soft rug.

But when I looked in the obvious spots—bedside
table, dresser top, your L-shaped jacket hook—the headphones didn't turn up.

Okay, please don't be mad, but that's when I looked in your closet. I didn't see my headphones draped on a hanger or hanging out of a pocket or anything . . . so I dug deeper.

Okay, please don't be mad again, but I looked at the shelves in the back of your closet. Right . . . the ones where you keep the secret things you think I don't know about, like your journals and the baby doll you pretended you gave away in first grade. I know, Lou. It's okay.

Okay, so please don't be mad *now,* but that's when I found it. Iris was beside me, wondering what I was doing on my hands and knees, and she started sniffing around at a particular box. A box that had a Post-it on it saying:

Louisa's Private Property
Do Not Open

(Here's a word of advice, Lou: If you don't want someone nosing around in something private, don't label it that way. Make it look really boring and no one will care. You'd be surprised what's hiding in my room in plain sight. Writing *private* and *do not open* on something is practically an invitation for people to snoop.)

So . . . okay, try not to be mad at this either, but I opened it. (Come on, how could I not?) And that's when I found your . . . what would you call it? Your collection? It doesn't seem right to call it a box of dirt and rocks, because there was a lot more to it than that. I couldn't believe the way you made something that messy so neat, with all the ziplock bags and the labels on them:

ORCHARD PARK on a bag of dirt.

LONGWOOD BEACH on a bag of sand.

BACKYARD BY IRIS'S DOG LEAD on another bag of dirt.

FINLEY'S GRAVEL on the bag of pink gravel.

I looked at the box lid again, and noticed something written on the lid under your *Do Not Open* Post-it. It looked like a math problem, only with names instead of numbers:

Louisa
Augusta
Mom
Dad
Iris
Finley
_____
Family

It didn't make a whole lot of sense, but I think I knew what it meant to you. I knew because it meant the same thing to me. Somehow, in that box of dirt, sand, and rocks from all the places that were important to us, we were all still together. We were still the old us. (Plus one new fish.)

That's when I knew I'd been getting you wrong, Lou. I thought nothing bothered you, but all along you'd been trying to find a way we could still be together. I get that now. So I hope you aren't too mad at me about going through your stuff. I put it all back the way it was.

# 41. The school custodian

I tried sneaking downstairs to look for my headphones in the living room, but Dad intercepted me in the foyer.

"Come here a minute, Gus," he said, heading back toward the kitchen.

"I don't feel like talking anymore."

"Then Mom and I will talk," he said. "Come on. I think you might like what we have to say."

Mom was pouring herself some tea as I stepped slowly into the kitchen. "Want some?" she asked as she looked up at me.

"No thanks. What's going on?" Whatever they had to say to me, I wanted them to get on with it. Even if Dad was saying I would like it. I'd be the judge of that.

"We believe you," Mom said. "We believe that you didn't do the graffiti."

"Okaaaay," I said. "Did someone else admit they did it?"

"No," Dad said. "But we trust you. You didn't lie about the gambling stuff, and we don't think you're lying about this."

"Okay, well . . . thanks. Does that mean I'm not punished?"

"Not by us," Mom said. "But you still have to do detention at school. And help clean up the graffiti. That was part of the deal."

"But how is that fair? What good is it for you guys to believe me if I'm still going to be punished?"

"Well, we hoped you'd be happy just to know we believe you," Dad said. "And we can try to talk to Mr. Smeed and plead your case. But we know he can be a tough customer, so we don't want you to get your hopes up."

That was something, at least. But I wasn't just worried for myself.

"What about my friends?" I asked.

"What about them?" Dad said. "Which friends?"

"Sarah and Nick and Syd and Elaine," I said, realizing as I said it that they all really were my friends. I mean, obviously Sarah was, but I don't think I knew that the others were too until I actually named them for Mom and Dad.

"We can't speak for them," Dad said. "Besides, how do you know they didn't do it?"

"I just know they wouldn't! And they were with me the whole time I was in the courtyard on Friday! No one was painting anything!"

"Okay, okay," Mom said in the voice she uses when one of us gets worked up. "We can ask Mr. Smeed about them too. I'll call him in the morning."

"I wish we could tell them who *did* do it," I said. "He doesn't even care about finding out the truth."

"Do you know who might have done it?" Dad asked.

"Sarah and I have some theories," I said. We'd been texting about it.

"Such as?"

"Well, Davis Davis has had a locker full of white paint all week for this JROTC project he's doing."

"Who?" Mom asked.

"Davis Davis. That's his real name. But I don't think it was him. I know he thinks I'm annoying, but he would never be so mean. Or break school rules that way."

I ventured forth my real theory: "I think it was one of the Silver Sisters. So does Sarah."

"*Who?*" Mom asked again.

"Yeah," Dad said, "who are all these people?"

"These aren't really people who matter," I said. "It's not like they're *my people.*" Now I was talking like Ms. Barakat without even thinking about it.

"Who are *your people* these days?" Mom asked. "You haven't talked much about anything all school year."

"You know," I said. "Sarah. Nick. This kid Elaine."

"Nick Zambrano?" Dad asked. "He's your person now?"

"Ugh, Dad, you know what I mean. No, he's not *my person.* He's just one of my friends. And like me, he's in trouble for something he didn't do."

"Okay," Dad said, "I hear you. And we will talk to Mr. Smeed. But you should still plan on doing detention after school tomorrow, in case we aren't able to convince him."

"Do I still have to pay for the supplies with my own money?"

Mom and Dad shared a quick look. "No," Mom said. "We can take care of that."

"Okay, good." I started wondering what exactly was involved with getting graffiti off a brick wall. I hoped I wouldn't have to find out.

"Hey, Gus," Mom said, crossing her arms and looking at a spot on the ceiling for a second, "you were right about something else."

"What do you mean?"

"About us," she answered. "Me and Dad. We haven't done the best job of communicating this year. And you're right: it hasn't been fair to you and Louie." She took a deep breath. "Especially the news about Mr. Singer," she said. "I definitely should have told Dad that first. And not asked you to keep it a secret."

"Okay," I said. Then I felt a little uneasy. "Is there anything else you guys need to tell each other? I mean, I don't have to hear it; I just want to make sure."

This time Dad sighed. "Yes," he said. "You might as well all know. I am going on tour with Spoiler Alert next summer. I am one of their new backup dancers."

Mom almost spit out her tea. "That is perfect for you, Matt," she said. "I know you'll make us proud."

Even I had to laugh at that one. Dad can be pretty good at breaking up a tense moment.

Mom rinsed out her teacup. "I have to go pick up Louie at after-school soon," she said, glancing at the clock on the microwave. "And I have no idea what we're having for dinner." Then she switched from her talking-to-herself voice to a voice that seemed more awkward.

"Do you . . . want to have takeout with us?" she

asked, looking at Dad. I think she wasn't sure if either of them were ready for family dinner yet after all the stuff that had happened Friday with Mr. Singer, the WOLD van, and the police-station visit.

Dad paused for a second and looked at me. "Okay, sure," he said. "Pizza?"

"Actually," I said, "what about Chicken Shack? For Louie? It's her favorite, and I think it's her turn to choose. And maybe after that we can play Garbage with her? You know she always wants to."

It wasn't your turn to choose the takeout place, Lou. It was my turn. And as you know, I hate Chicken Shack. But after seeing your little shoebox of rocks, sand, and dirt . . . well, what can I say? I was in the mood to let you have your way.

Dad looked at me like he didn't know who I was. "Are you serious?"

"That's awfully generous of you," Mom said.

"Hey," I said as I grabbed a pre-dinner apple from the fruit bowl. "I *told* you I wasn't a bad kid."

. . .

The next morning, I had a text from Layla:

*Guinea pig!*

She also sent a picture of her grinning and holding a little chocolate-brown ball of fluff.

I texted back:

*OMG*

Layla had wanted a guinea pig forever. We had talked about it so many times—and her parents had said no so many times—that it had come to feel like a silly dream, like talking about going to the moon.

Layla's next text was *Her name is Officer Nibbles. Come meet her after school!*

And I wanted to. I *really* wanted to. I know I didn't want to talk to Layla about schools or friends or dances or any of those things these days, but I knew where I stood with Layla on the subject of guinea pigs. She wanted one. I wanted her to have one. I was genuinely happy for her.

But of course I couldn't go to Layla's after school. Not that day. No, I had detention for something I hadn't done. And more than ever, I was wondering one thing: Who *did* do it? Who had painted those pictures and made us all get detention from Smeed?

Those were the things I was still wondering as I stood in the courtyard after school that day with Sarah, Nick, Syd, and Elaine. We'd all been instructed to bring a snack to eat before we got started. I had a granola bar; Sarah

had popcorn; Syd, of course, had a tomato; and Nick had a bag of potato chips. Elaine didn't have anything.

"I forgot about the snack," she said quietly, and Nick and Sarah nudged her on both her elbows and offered her popcorn and chips at the same time.

"Good luck with your new job!" a voice called from the courtyard doorway. It was Addison, standing with Heidi and Marcy. She was using the kind of singsong voice I use with Ama when I'm trying to get her to cooperate.

"Sorry you have to get rid of that fantastic mural," Heidi added.

"I can't believe she knows the word 'mural,'" I muttered to Sarah.

"I can't believe she knows the word 'fantastic,'" Sarah muttered back.

"Come on—I have to go, you guys," Marcy said, starting down the hall away from her friends. It was the first time I'd seen her do something without waiting for Addison to take the lead. Addison waited a beat and waved at us, then went the way Marcy had gone. And of course Heidi followed.

"Okay, boys and girls, time for Graffiti Cleaning 101," Mr. Solo said. Mr. Solo is the school custodian. I'd seen him in the hallways and the cafeteria, but had never

talked to him before. He's someone the teachers always refer to when they're reminding us what slobs we are. ("Do not leave the classroom looking like this; Mr. Solo should not have to deal with this mess!" or "Mr. Solo is not your parent; do not expect him to clean up after you!" which is always kind of funny to me since my parents definitely don't want me to think they'll clean up my messes either.)

Considering how tough the teachers always make Mr. Solo's life sound, I was surprised to discover that he seemed like a pretty cheery guy. Definitely happier than some of the teachers who yell about him.

"The first thing you will need is gloves." Mr. Solo started handing bright orange rubber gloves to each of us. "Because we are using chemicals that you do not— I repeat, *do not*—want to get on your skin. I'll be right back."

Syd looked nervous. "Is this okay?" he said as Mr. Solo started rummaging through the supply cart he'd left by the courtyard door. "I mean, it doesn't seem safe for kids to use chemicals like that. Sarah, isn't your mom a lawyer?"

Sarah gave him a pitying look. "No. She's an accountant."

"Gus's mom is an ER nurse," Nick said. "That could

come in handy." He smiled; he didn't look nearly as nervous as Syd did.

"Okay, here we are." Mr. Solo returned with an armful of spray cans. "This is your first weapon." He held up a can for us to see; it was something called Graffiti Delete.

"And this is your second weapon." He held out a box of steel-wool pads and told us to each take one.

"First you spray; then you scrub. As hard as you can. For a while. If that doesn't do it, spray and scrub again. Any questions?"

"Yeah, I have a question," Nick said. "What if we're here for no reason? What if we aren't the ones who did the graffiti?"

Mr. Solo looked at us for a second, then shrugged and raised his hands in the air. "I suppose that is between you and Mr. Smeed. Or between you and the kids who actually did it. You could also look at it this way: Maybe you *are* here for a reason. Even if you didn't do it. Think about what that reason might be."

"To . . . learn how to clean graffiti?" Syd asked. Nick snorted.

Mr. Solo smiled. "Maybe that," he said. "Maybe something else."

He took a bucket off the supply cart and headed

toward the door. "But for now, *my* reason for being here is to make sure the school gets cleaned up. So if you have any questions, look for me in the gym; I'll be in there polishing the floors."

He left us to our work.

# 42. The SS 1400

"So. How should we split this up?" Sarah asked, pulling on her gloves.

"Well, we each actually have our name under one of the characters," Syd said. "Why don't we just take our own?"

"I don't know." I said. "That feels like admitting that we are who this says we are. Know what I mean? I think we should mix it up."

"I agree with Gus," Nick said. "Take someone else's drawing."

"Okay," Syd shrugged. "I'll do yours, Sarah."

Syd went over to the Sarah caricature and started spraying Graffiti Delete on it. Sarah did the same to the Syd character.

Elaine looked at me like she was waiting to be told where to go. "Want to switch?" I asked her.

"Hey, wait—that means I'm the only one doing my own cartoon," Nick said.

"Oh, right. Okay, Nick does Elaine's, Elaine does mine, and I'll do yours," I said. Nick nodded, and went to work on Elaine's caricature. Elaine walked over to start on mine. I gave it one last glance before she got started. I always wondered how I looked to other people—was this the answer? Ugh, these stupid glasses.

"Remind me again why we're doing this?" Syd asked after he finished spraying "Sarah's" head and long hair with Graffiti-be-Gone.

"Because Smeed's a jerk and won't listen to us," I said. Smeed had been gone for the first part of homeroom. This was unusual lately. I think that after the Binaca incident, Principal Olin must have talked to him about leaving the class unattended, because it never happened anymore. And that was probably another reason he seemed to have it out for the kids in his homeroom. We hadn't just gotten ourselves in trouble on Binaca Day; we'd gotten him in trouble too.

So this morning, when Smeed was gone and Ms.

Vanwickle, the serious lunch aide, was asked to monitor our classroom for a while, everyone knew he must be gone for a real reason. And I knew what the reason was: he was meeting with my parents so they could plead my innocence. I hadn't told anyone but Sarah, and she'd said her mom was going to send an email too. But something about your parents making a special trip to school to talk to your teacher feels more embarrassing in middle school than it does in elementary school.

Anyway, I was glad I decided not to tell anyone about their meeting, because it didn't work. Smeed came to the classroom five minutes before the end of the period with an even bigger smirk on his face than usual, and he handed me an envelope. I tried to open it without anyone noticing, but I could tell Nick was peering over at me.

I pulled a piece of paper out of the envelope and saw Mom's familiar neat cursive writing:

*Hey, Gus—*

*I promise we tried our best, but Mr. Smeed wouldn't budge. He doesn't believe us, or at least he doesn't want to. Principal Olin was in another meeting, but I'm going to send her an email when I get a break at work.*

*In the meantime, I'm sorry you still have*
*to do detention today. We believe you and*
*we love you, and Dad will pick you up at 5.*
*(We know you'll be tired, so you don't have*
*to walk home today.)*
                              *Love,*
                              *Mom*

And in boxier letters at the bottom:


*(and Dad)*


Now, scrubbing away at cartoon "Nick's" spiky hair on the courtyard wall, I felt like the steel-wool pad was chanting as it moved against the bricks: *We didn't do it. We didn't do it. We didn't do it.* Sometimes I shifted my rhythm so it sounded more like *This is so unfair. This is so unfair. This is so unfair.*

"This is so unfair," a voice said behind me. I jumped a little; it was like someone had heard my secret scrubbing chant.

I turned around and saw Quincy standing with her arms crossed, watching us. "It's so obvious you guys didn't do this," she said. "Why would anyone draw these stupid pictures of themselves?"

She bent down and picked up the extra pair of gloves. "I'll help you guys," she said. "Is anyone doing the names?"

"Not yet," Sarah said. "And thanks." I could tell she was surprised; I'm not sure she'd ever seen the helpful side of Quincy before.

"Sure," Quincy said. "It helps if you spray the cleaner on the wall *and* the steel wool. Although it would be way easier if they let you use a power sprayer. That's the best way to do it."

"How do you know that?" Nick asked.

Quincy smiled at him. "Don't you worry about that, Zambrano."

She sprayed some Graffiti Delete on the *E* in *Elaine*. "I just can't believe you guys are taking this," she said.

"What can we even do about it?" Sarah asked. "No one believes us."

"Actually . . . ," I said, "my parents believe me." I felt a little bolder admitting that, knowing Quincy believed us too. "But it doesn't matter."

"Did they come to school to try to bail you out?" Nick asked. "I saw them going into the office this morning."

I wondered if he'd also read Mom's letter over my

shoulder. "Well, not just me," I said. "All of us. I told them none of us did it."

"You're lucky," Elaine said. "My parents didn't believe me at all."

"Mine neither," said Nick.

I wasn't sure what to say. "Maybe my parents could talk to them too?" I offered.

"I just want to find out who *did* do it," Nick said. "Then everyone will believe us."

"Not necessarily," Syd said. "Not if we don't have proof."

"See that?" Quincy asked, pointing toward the top of a courtyard wall. "Your proof is right there."

I looked where she was pointing. I couldn't believe it. How had I never noticed it before?

"Holy crap," Nick said. "It's a camera." He squinted to read the small print below it. "SS 1400 Security System. It's a security camera."

"It sure is," Quincy said. "And it points right at this wall."

She stood up straight and stopped spraying. "Think we should take a break and visit Ms. Olin?"

■ ■ ■

We couldn't do anything about the camera until the next day. Nick ran down the hall to ask Principal Olin if we could see the video from the security camera, but she was already gone for the day. When he got back, Quincy took off her gloves and looked at us.

"You guys, you really should quit until they know who did this. Go on strike until you get a fair trial."

"Quincy's right," I said. "Why should we keep working if there's a chance we can prove our innocence?" I took off my gloves too and sat on a bench.

When Mr. Solo came to check on our progress, we were all sitting on the ground or on benches. I was eating my granola bar. Elaine, Sarah, and Quincy were braiding blades of grass into bracelets. Syd and Nick were throwing crab apples into Syd's hat.

"How's it going out here, people?" Mr. Solo peered through the courtyard door and saw us all sitting down. He stepped the rest of the way in and looked at the wall, which now had five headless characters and five names on it (one of the names was now *laine,* since Quincy had erased the first *E*). He looked at Quincy. "Why are you here? I left five kids working, and I came back to six kids having a party." Some party this would be.

"Quincy was helping us," I said. "She scrubbed the *E.*"

"Well, that's very kind of her. But why isn't anyone doing anything now?"

"We're on strike." I tried to say it with the same amount of force Quincy had used a minute ago.

"What was that?" It's possible Mr. Solo hadn't understood me because the word "strike" had come out as a whisper.

"Strike," Quincy said. "It means they won't work until their demands are met."

"I know what a strike is," Mr. Solo said. "I just couldn't hear her. But I'm not sure what you kids are driving at. What are your demands?"

"We demand that we not have to do any more cleanup until someone listens to us and believes that we didn't do it," Nick said. "We have proof."

"What kind of proof?"

All six of us pointed up at the security camera at the exact same time.

"Aha," Mr. Solo said. He looked at the camera for several seconds, then back at us. "You guys really didn't do this, did you?"

Sarah and Elaine shook their heads. The rest of us shouted, "NO!"

"I believe you," Mr. Solo said. "But it'll take some doing to get Ms. Olin to crack open that camera for the footage. I think they have to involve the police if they want to watch it."

"That's fine by us," Syd said. "We're innocent!"

"Okay, okay," Mr. Solo said. "You can go home. I'll talk to Ms. Olin for you and we'll see what we can do about this tomorrow."

# 43. Keira

Nick's brother, Moe, gave me a ride home. I had texted Dad to pick me up, but since we were done early, he was stuck in a meeting at work and asked if I could wait. I really didn't feel like being at school a half second longer so I took Nick up on his offer to ride with him.

Moe has always been kind of fascinating to me. Did you know his real name is Morris? He's five years older than Nick and me and he never hung out with the neighborhood kids our age when we were younger and running lemonade stands or building tree forts. I don't know if you ever noticed, Louie; you were pretty little when we were doing that stuff. Moe would ride by on his bike or skateboard sometimes, either with friends or by himself. Most of the time he was listening to music on headphones and ignored us; sometimes he'd flash us a peace sign or take out one earbud and talk to us for a minute while he bought lemonade. Last year he got his driver's license, so we don't see him on his bike anymore. And I guess we aren't doing lemonade stands or tree forts anymore either. But if he sees me in our yard he'll still flash me a little peace sign. Even if he doesn't look at me or lift his dark sunglasses, I feel like he's still a pretty cool guy, as older teenage brothers go.

And here's some news: I think he has a girlfriend. Because when he came to school to pick us up, there was a girl in the car with him.

"Hey, Gus," Moe said. "Gus, meet Keira. Keira, Gus." Keira turned around and gave us a little wave.

"Hey, Keira," Nick said, and she said "Hey, Nick" back in a way that made me think they'd been around each other a bunch of times before. When Keira turned around, I looked at Nick and mouthed, *Girlfriend?* and he shrugged in a way that seemed more like a yes than a no.

Keira's dark hair was on top of her head in a crazy bun that would have looked messy or goofy on most people, but somehow made her look cool. She had dangly beaded earrings and—get this—big glasses with thick black frames. And somehow those looked cool too. Glasses.

"Did you get glasses?" Nick asked her. "I've never seen you wear them before."

"They're fake," Moe said. "She has perfect vision but she wanted to be able to see through things like Superman."

Keira gave him a light slap on the arm. "I just like the way they look. Gus knows what I mean, right?" She looked at me like we were in a high-fashion-glasses conspiracy together.

"I guess?" I said. But I knew I couldn't really fake it in front of Nick and Moe, who knew I'd had glasses most of my life. "I mean, actually, mine are real. I've always had them."

"Ack, you're so lucky! I've been wanting to get them forever, but my mom said she wasn't going to spend money on something 'frivolous' like that, so I saved my babysitting money to get the frames I wanted."

Ironic, right? I was babysitting to pay for contacts, and Keira had used her babysitting money to pay for glasses.

"I like your frames too, though," she said. "I like how they're rounder than mine."

"Yeah, I like Gus's glasses too," Nick said. He was looking out the car window, and his voice was so low I could barely hear him. I looked over and saw that his ears looked a little red. Maybe he didn't want Moe to hear him say something nice to a girl?

"So how come you guys keep getting in trouble this year?" Moe's voice didn't sound like he was making fun of us; he seemed genuinely curious.

"It's Smeed," Nick said. "He has it out for us."

"Ugh, I had him in sixth grade," Keira said. "He's the worst. Does he still spray Binaca in his mouth all day long?"

"Yeah," Nick said.

"Want to tell us more about that, Nicky?" Moe tried to catch Nick's eye in the rearview mirror. And okay, this time it did seem like he was making fun of us a little.

"No, we're all set," Nick said.

"So what do you mean he has it out for you?" Keira asked. "Are you getting in trouble for stuff you didn't do?"

"Yes!" I said. I didn't wait for Nick to answer; I was dying to talk about Smeed with someone older than us who knew what he was like. "He thinks we painted graffiti in the courtyard. Stupid pictures of ourselves. Why would we do that?"

"So who did do it?"

"We're trying to find out," Nick said. "Tomorrow

we're gonna ask Ms. Olin if she can check the security cameras."

"But Mr. Solo said they have to ask the police," I said. "Do you think that's true?"

"Yeah, maybe," Moe said. "Evidence of a crime and all? I don't know."

"Who do you *think* did it?" Keira asked.

"What about that Gosley jerk?" Nick said. "The one who pinches all the girls?"

Keira's head whipped around. "What do you mean, 'pinches all the girls'?"

"That's exactly what he means," I said. "This guy roams the school and pinches us on our butts. Hard. People call him the Gooser. Although I haven't heard of him doing it since Nick yelled at him at the dance. And El . . . and someone tripped him." I almost forgot Elaine wanted to stay anonymous.

"That's crazy," Keira said. "That's actually assault. Has anyone reported him?"

Wow. "Assault" sounded much worse than "pinching." I didn't know what to say. I guess Keira could tell the answer was no.

"Okay, Gus, you should just know that's really bad and he shouldn't be allowed to get away with it. You guys should tell someone. Definitely if he does it again."

"Okay," I said. "I guess I didn't see much point; I didn't think it would change anything."

Nick looked serious now too. "Promise you'll say something if he does it again?" he asked.

"Yes, okay," I said. I suddenly really wanted to change the subject. I didn't like thinking there was yet another thing this year I'd handled badly. Even if it really wasn't my fault.

"Anyway, back to the graffiti," I said. I looked at Nick. He hadn't heard Sarah's and my theory yet. "I think it was some girls in our grade. I think it was Addison and those guys. Heidi and Marcy."

"Didn't you used to be friends with Marcy?" Nick asked. "What happened?"

"I don't know," I said, which was the truth. "I mean, last year she kind of annoyed me because she wanted to hang out all the time, so I tried to keep my distance from her. And then this year everything was different. *She* was different."

"Well, she probably got tired of trying to hang out with you and getting shot down," Nick said.

"Geez, Nick, don't give Gus a guilt trip," Keira said. "Sometimes friendships just change."

"Thanks," I said. Although I did wonder sometimes if Marcy was mad at me for not hanging out as much as she wanted to last year. Or maybe she just realized she fit in more with Addison and her gang after she grew a foot and got into makeup and jewelry over the summer in Canada. Maybe a little of both.

"Here you go, Gus," Moe said, pulling up in front of our house.

"Thanks for the ride."

I got out of the car and started walking up our front steps.

"Hey, wait a sec!" It was Nick, chasing after me with my hoodie, which I'd left in the car.

He caught up to me and handed me the hoodie.

"Tomorrow we get vindicated," he said.

"Ha, so dramatic," I said. "But I hope you're right."

"Well, either way, it was fun serving time together. Again." Nick smiled. "And hey—even if she is being a jerk this year, I kind of feel bad for Marcy. I mean, I'm not sure what I'd do if you started trying to cut *me* loose."

"Nick-ay! We're moving out!" Moe yelled.

Nick gave me a little wave, then turned and trotted back down the step.

And okay, Louie, I'll admit it: I think that time maybe *my* ears turned a little red.

# 44. Officer Delgado

I was only in homeroom for about thirty seconds the next morning before Ms. Vanwickle showed up and said she would watch the class again because Mr. Smeed was needed in Principal Olin's office.

"I'm sure some of us can guess what this is about," Smeed said, looking at Nick and me as he smoothed down his tie. "I happened to glance into the court-yard this morning. Not exactly a stellar cleanup job, was it?"

Nick looked at me and raised his eyebrows. I knew what he was thinking: Smeed didn't know about the security camera yet. I pictured him walking into Ms. Olin's office and being confronted by a police officer who was broadcasting video of the real perpetrators on the office wall.

*Look what you've done!* Ms. Olin would shout. *We have persecuted innocent children because of your false accusations!*

I know that was probably a lot to hope for. But ten minutes later, when Nick and I were called into Ms. Olin's office, there was an actual police officer sitting there. (I realize this brings the total number of police officers I've met during my first year of middle school to three. And it's only November. I hope your tally is considerably lower, Lou.)

The policeman and Ms. Olin weren't the only people in the room. Mr. Wyatt and Mr. Solo were there too, and so were Smeed, Elaine, Sarah, and Syd. In fact, there were so many people that they weren't sitting in Ms. Olin's actual office; instead, everyone was gathered in the waiting area outside her office. And since this area has big windows that look onto the main hallway, you can imagine how many people were slowing down and staring. It was like we were in a giant fishbowl. With the principal, assistant principal, and a police officer. I think a circus would have drawn less attention.

"Come in," Mr. Wyatt said, hitching his khaki pants even higher than usual over his Meridian Middle School golf shirt. I walked in as Rob Vinson was slowing down and peering in at the crowd. "You're going in there,

Little Gus?" he asked. "Good luck!" He gave me a light chuck on the shoulder.

"Mr. Zambrano, Ms. Reynolds, there are seats right up here," Mr. Wyatt said. Great. Since we were the last ones to arrive, we had to sit in the front. Nick and I squeezed past the other kids to get to two folding chairs right by the front desk. There we had a perfect view of the police officer, who was fiddling with some electronic equipment.

"This is Officer Delgado," Principal Olin said. "He's going to see if the footage from the camera in the courtyard can help us get to the bottom of the graffiti situation."

Officer Delgado looked up from the ancient-looking black box on the desk in front of him and gave us all a small nod. The look on his face reminded me of Dad when he's trying to figure out why the printer is glitching. It was the face of someone who would prefer not to have an audience while he tackles a frustrating problem.

Nick must have felt bad for Officer Delgado too, because he raised his hand and asked, "So . . . you haven't watched the video yet?"

"No one has," Officer Delgado said. "The camera is about twenty years old and it's seen some weather. I'm working on it."

"To be honest," said Principal Olin, "we'd forgotten the camera was there. It was installed long before I was principal here, and I've never had to use it. But in any event, we thought we'd ask you all here in case there's anything you need to tell us while we wait," Principal Olin said. "Mr. Solo says you have reason to believe this video will exonerate you." I think she could tell by our faces that we weren't sure what that meant. "Clear your names. Prove your innocence."

"It will," Nick said. "But if you can't get the video to work, does that mean we're still punished?"

She didn't have a chance to answer. "You don't have to watch the video," a shaky voice from the back of the room said. "I can tell you who did it."

# 45. The Vandal

All the bodies in the room turned at once, the way the seagulls at Longwood Beach all pivot in our direction whenever one of us opens a bag of pretzels. But this distraction was way more interesting than a bag of pretzels. This was Marcy, standing in the doorway and looking at the floor as she fiddled with an earring. Not a silver hoop, I noticed, but a small gold butterfly. I wondered why no silver today.

"Come in, Marcy," Principal Olin said. Marcy ventured a few small steps forward, but with the room as packed as it was, it was hard for her to get all the way to the front.

"What is it, Miss Shea?" Mr. Wyatt boomed across the room. "You have something to tell us?"

Marcy looked up at him, and I could see her face was red and her eyes were shiny. She was scared. Principal Olin must have noticed too, because she said, "Actually, Mr. Wyatt, perhaps we should speak with Marcy in private."

She opened her office door and waved Marcy, Mr. Wyatt, and Officer Delgado in.

"*I knew it!*" Syd whisper-hissed as soon as the door was closed.

"Knew what?" Sarah whispered back.

"It was those girls! Those silver girls or whatever you call them. They would totally do something like this. They're just mean."

He was right, of course. He was right about all of it. But I knew Sarah was thinking the same thing I was thinking: that it was too much to hope Marcy was swooping in with a confession. That she would actually throw herself and her Silver Sisters on the mercy of the principals and the police in order to save us.

As we'd soon find out, we were on target with one thing. Marcy wasn't turning in the names of her friends. She was only turning in herself.

■ ■ ■

"You're kidding," Mom said when I called from the office phone to tell her I didn't have to repeat detention that day after all.

"Nope. After Marcy left the office, Ms. Olin came out and apologized to us—me, Sarah, Nick, Elaine, and Syd. She said they had new information that cleared our names, and that we didn't have to finish the cleanup."

"And the new information was from Marcy?"

"Well, Ms. Olin didn't say that, but she didn't have to. This happened right after Marcy went into her office."

"So *Marcy* did the graffiti?"

"Yeah, she must have. I'm sure it was her and Addison and Heidi. Probably Amber too."

"Wasn't Heidi the one who refused to do the Binaca bet because she wouldn't gamble?" Mom asked.

"Yeah, but Addison wasn't there when that happened," I explained. "She'll do anything Addison says."

"I see," Mom said. "Well, this is who you suspected all along, isn't it?" Mom asked.

"Pretty much."

"Wow. Well, I'm glad you've been cleared, but I'm sorry to hear that about Marcy."

"Yeah."

"What did Mr. Smeed say?"

"Not much. He doesn't like being wrong."

"Yeah, I suspect he doesn't. Oh, hey"—Mom remembered something—"now that you don't have detention after school today, can you go over to Ama's? Dr. Chen texted me and said she could use the help."

"Okay, sure."

"How close are you to your contact-lens goal?" Mom asked. "I thought I'd see if Dr. Sherman could see you in the next couple of weeks. Maybe Dad and I can even foot part of the bill for you."

I looked up and saw Syd making a circling *Get on with it* motion with his hand; he was waiting to call his parents.

"Sure, Mom, but I have to get going now. I'm on the office phone."

"Okay, hon. Dr. Chen will text you when she's on her way to pick you up."

As I handed the phone receiver to Syd, I did some calculations in my head. Mom and Dad wouldn't even have to contribute that much to round out the amount I needed for contacts. I couldn't wait to tell Sarah.

There was one more thing I needed to do before I left the office. I'd been thinking about what Keira had said about the Gooser, and about how he shouldn't be allowed to get away with hurting so many people. I took a blank piece of paper from the front desk and wrote a quick note:

*Dear Principal Olin,*
　　*I think you should know that Ronald Gosley pinches girls' bottoms in school. And out of school too. A lot. It hurts. Someone should do something about it. Thanks.*

I slid the note into Principal Olin's office mailbox. I didn't sign it. I guess I was afraid of what might happen if he found out I was the one who reported him. But at least I'd done something. Keira was right. Someone had to.

# 46. The rat(s)

I had to wait until lunch to tell Sarah the good news about my contact-lens fund. She had already been shooed out of the office by the school secretary, Ms. Wester, and now Ms. Wester was shooing me to first period.

Sarah was waiting in the hall by the courtyard at lunchtime. "Do you want to eat there today?" she asked. "You know, with the graffiti still on the wall?"

I looked through the doorway at the pitiful headless characters. I wasn't sure. Would it be like we were sitting there with a mark on us for everyone to see? Like a KICK ME sign on our backs, only way bigger?

"Why are you guys just standing here?" Nick gave my ponytail a little tug as he zipped past into the courtyard.

"Come on, I'm starving." Another zip from Syd, joining Nick by the crab apple tree.

"Okay . . . ," Sarah said. "We just aren't sure about eating out here with . . . that."

"What, the 'fantastic mural'?" Nick called from the tree. "Come on, who cares about that anymore?"

"Yeah," Syd said. "Besides, it'll be gone tomorrow after Marcy does her detention this afternoon." He gave a little cackle.

"Come on," I said to Sarah. As usual, the thought of eating in the courtyard—even with the graffiti on the wall—was better than facing Addison and Heidi and their crowd in the cafeteria.

"Where's Elaine?" Sarah asked as we stepped through the courtyard door.

"I'm here." Elaine popped up behind us, a little pink-faced and out of breath. I was glad she'd heard Sarah asking where she was. I think she needed re-assurance that we actually did want to hang out with her.

"Oh, hey," Sarah said. "Why are you all out of breath?"

"I just ran here from where I was hiding under the stairwell."

"Why were you hiding under the stairwell?" I was a

little nervous to hear her answer. Elaine could be a question mark sometimes.

"Well, I was kind of eavesdropping. On Marcy and Addison. They were talking about the graffiti."

This got the boys' attention. "What were they saying?" Nick asked.

"Marcy was saying something about how it wasn't right that we were being punished, and Addison said something like 'Who cares? It's not like those losers have anything better to do.'

"Then Marcy said, 'You know what I mean, Addison.' And you know how Addison is usually all cool, like she doesn't care about anything? She wasn't that way just now. She was like, 'You better not say another word to anyone about this, Marcy.'

"Then Marcy said, 'I *told* you, Addison; I didn't say anything about you guys. *I'm* the one doing detention. You're safe.' "

"Then what?" I asked.

"Then nothing. I heard one of them start to walk down the stairs, and that's when I ran here."

"Wow. So what does it mean?" Syd asked.

"It means Addison's not getting in trouble even though she was part of it," I said. "Knowing her, it was probably all her idea. But Marcy wouldn't tell on her."

"Too scared of her, probably," Syd said.

"Or just didn't want to rat out her friend," said Elaine.

"Ugh, but Addison already is such a rat herself." Sarah rolled her eyes. "That news has been out for a while."

...

Language arts felt different that day. Addison and Heidi walked in without Marcy. She arrived alone a few minutes later, and they didn't even say hi to her. When she went to her seat, they twisted toward each other like snakes. As they whispered and shot occasional glances at Marcy, she faced away from them, looking out the window as she fiddled with one of her butterfly earrings again. They were still wearing their silver hoops.

If Ms. Barakat noticed anything was off, she didn't show it. At least not right away.

"Okay, class," she said, firing up her laptop. "Today a new poem. 'Mariposa' by Edna St. Vincent Millay. *Mariposa* is a Spanish word. Who knows what it means?"

She looked around the room, and her eyes landed

on Marcy. "Ooh, a clue!" she said. "Someone has little *mariposas* on her ears!"

Marcy put her hands up to her earrings again. "Me?" she said. "Oh . . . b-butterflies?" From the way she stumbled on the word, I could tell she wasn't sure she had the right answer. And Addison and Heidi thought this was uproariously funny.

It was hard to tell what happened first, but in the space of a few seconds, Addison mimicked "b-butterflies," Heidi started choking because she couldn't hold back her cackling, and Marcy's hand shot into the air.

"Ms. Barakat," she said in a strangled voice without waiting to be called on, "I need to go to the bathroom."

"Of course, Marcy, go ahead." Ms. Barakat looked at Addison and Heidi as Marcy walked out. She took a deep breath as she clicked on her laptop to put the poem on the Smart Board. "Addison, can you read the first stanza, please?"

As Addison took a deep breath to clear her giggles before she read, Ms. Barakat held up her right hand as though she'd just had another thought. "Also, can you and Heidi please stay after class for a few minutes?"

Addison gave a little nod and started reading. Heidi turned about ten different shades of red.

...

Marcy still wasn't back fifteen minutes later, and Ms. Barakat sent me to the bathroom to check on her. I wasn't sure I was the best choice for that job, given all that was going on with the graffiti that week, but it didn't seem like a great time to argue with Ms. Barakat.

When I walked into the bathroom, only one stall was occupied. I peeked under the door and saw Marcy's black ankle boots. I cleared my throat a little.

"Marcy?"

No answer.

"Hey, Marcy, I know you're here. Ms. Barakat wanted me to check and make sure you're okay. It's Augusta."

"I *know* it's you, Augusta."

"Oh, okay. Well, um . . . are you okay?"

"Yes, I'm great."

"Okay . . . I'll let her know."

I couldn't just leave, though. Of course I knew she wasn't really great. But I also didn't know what to say next. Part of me felt like I should thank her for admitting to the graffiti and getting us off the hook, but why would I do that? Why would I thank her if she was the one who painted those stupid pictures in the first place? Why did she even do it? That's what I wanted to know first.

"Hey . . . Marcy . . . about the graffiti . . ."

"I didn't do it."

That wasn't what I'd expected to hear.

"What do you mean, you didn't do it? Everyone knows you did it. You told Ms. Olin you did it."

"I didn't do it. I know you didn't do it. And neither did I. And that's all I'll say."

"Wait . . . why are you doing detention if you didn't do it?" The stall door opened and Marcy stepped out. She was blowing her nose on a piece of toilet paper and her eyes were red; I could tell she'd been crying. She looked down as she threw the toilet paper away and washed her hands.

"I'm doing detention because I know who *did* do the graffiti," she said. "And I know it wasn't you guys. And it's not right for you to take the fall."

"Yeah, but it's not right for you to take the fall either if you didn't do it!" I said. "I know it was Addison and Heidi and Amber. *Everyone* knows. You're doing this so they won't get in trouble, aren't you?"

"I *said* I'm doing it so that you guys wouldn't have

to," Marcy said. "I'm trying to do something nice for you, if you'll let me. Geez, Augusta, does anyone ever know where they stand with you?"

I didn't know what to say to that, but it didn't matter. Marcy dried her hands, chucked the paper towel in the garbage, and walked out on her own. I wondered how long I could wait in the bathroom before Ms. Barakat sent someone to check on me.

# 47. The tough nut

"Ugh, Addison and Heidi are the *worst*," Sarah said in math after I told her about my bathroom conversation with Marcy. "Amber too. Why is Marcy even friends with them?"

"That's the thing . . . I don't know if she is anymore. They weren't talking to her in language arts. And she's not even wearing the silver hoops today. She said she did this for *us*, because it wasn't right that we were being punished for something we didn't do."

"Wow, seriously?"

"Yeah." I debated whether to tell Sarah the next part. "She said something else weird . . . that I wasn't letting her do a nice thing, and that people never know where they stand with me. What does that even mean?"

Sarah shrugged. "Well, you can be a tough nut to

crack sometimes. Like when Nick wanted you to dance, or what you told me about how you wouldn't let Quincy help you with your gym locker." *And how I never tell my little sister anything about middle school when she asks,* I silently added.

"Yeah, but you can sort of be like that too," I said. "Poor Syd, for example . . ."

She laughed. "I know. Maybe that's why we're friends."

I laughed too. But I was thinking of the one thing Sarah didn't know about how I was tough to crack. How I'd barely talked to you, Lou, about anything important all year.

⏺ ⏺ ⏺

"Okay, Miss Shea, time for Graffiti Cleaning 101," I heard as I walked past the courtyard door on my way out of the building that afternoon. Mr. Solo sounded more tired than he had with us yesterday. He probably hadn't counted on having to give the graffiti speech twice in as many days.

I didn't want to look into the courtyard. The easy thing to do would have been to speed up and zip down the hallway, out of the building, and into a sunny afternoon spent drinking pretend tea with Ama, Scooter, and Granola.

But I had to. I couldn't make my eyes go anywhere else but through the open courtyard door, which was where I saw Marcy, her back to me, putting on rubber gloves and nodding slowly as she listened to Mr. Solo's instructions. For the first time this year, she looked small, and very alone.

I pulled my phone out of my jacket pocket and texted Dr. Chen.

*Really sorry but I can't come over today after all. Is that ok?*

While I waited for her to respond, I texted Mom to let her know.

Dr. Chen texted me back: *No worries; hope everything is okay.*

Mom's text was a little less understanding: *Did you tell Dr. Chen? What's going on?*

I texted the same thing back to both of them:

*Yes. I just need to help a friend.*

■ ■ ■

"What are you doing?" Marcy asked when she noticed me behind her, putting on a pair of rubber gloves.

"I'm helping you."

"This isn't your job," she said. "You didn't make this mess."

"Yeah, but neither did you. So we'll just beautify the school together. Plus, I have experience now and I can give you tips. Like it's easier if you spray the wall *and* the steel wool with the cleaning stuff."

"Of course, what we really need is a power washer," a voice behind me said. I turned to see Sarah sliding her backpack off her shoulder and onto a bench. She held out her hand. "Gloves, please." Elaine was close behind her; after peering around the doorway, she waved and walked in to join Sarah at the supply cart.

"I thought you kids were off the hook for this," Mr. Solo said, wrinkling one eyebrow as he looked at Sarah, Elaine, and me.

"We are," said another new voice from the doorway. "But it's only right for us to help now that we're, like, graffiti-cleaning experts." It was Nick, followed immediately by Syd. They dropped their backpacks on the bench beside Sarah's.

"What, still no power washer?" Quincy was the last to arrive.

"Did you guys plan this?" Marcy asked.

"I don't know . . . *did* we?" Quincy asked, looking

274

around at the rest of us. "Or was it just our hive mind at work? Or . . . *did* we?" She gave a fake little cackle.

"You're weird," Marcy said. But she said it almost in an admiring voice, not the constantly critical voice she used with Addison and Heidi. It occurred to me that Marcy might actually still be trying to find her people too.

And I thought about what Quincy had said about our "hive mind." The truth was that we hadn't planned to meet out here. Maybe the others felt bad for Marcy like I did. Maybe they wanted to pitch in so we could help each other. Or maybe there was something to this *hive mind* business. And if it was, this hive also felt a lot like what Ms. Barakat might call a village.

"All right, then," Mr. Solo said. "I'm going to check on some loose masonry back here; then I'll leave you *experts* alone." The way he said it almost sounded like he thought we were crazy, but I saw a smile in his eyes as he ducked behind some bushes to check the crumbly bricks. I think Mr. Solo was proud of us. And that he could tell we were starting to form our village, or our hive. Maybe that was the real "reason for being here" he'd been talking about yesterday.

Then there was another voice from the doorway. This one wasn't nearly as welcome as the others had been.

"Hey, *losers* . . . you missed a spot!" Of course there was no need to turn around and see who'd said it. I'd know that dry, sarcastic tone anywhere. Same with the nervous giggle that followed it. Addison and Heidi.

"Oh, look, and there's a new loser today! Working hard with your new best friends, huh, Marcy?"

Marcy didn't turn around. She kept scrubbing, even as she blinked back tears.

"I'm sick of their crap," Sarah said. "Let's tell Mr. Solo; he's right there."

"Wait . . . ," I said as an idea occurred to me. Quincy must have thought the same thing, because she nodded and whispered, "Yeah, don't tell him. Not yet."

I glanced back into the thick bushes where Mr. Solo had gone to fix the wall. He had been leaning over and chipping away at a brick before Addison and Heidi arrived, but now he was standing up and looking in our direction. I made eye contact with him. I wanted to put my finger to my lips and make a shushing motion, but I didn't want Addison to get suspicious. (Also, it would have seemed out of line to do that to an adult at school.) Turns out I didn't need to. I tried to make what I thought was a pleading face, and Mr. Solo got it. He nodded silently and stayed where he was.

It was Quincy's turn to keep the ball rolling. "As long

as you guys are here, why don't you help out instead of just standing in the hall and barking at us?" she said.

Addison laughed. "Yeah, that's a hard pass. Pretty sure we have better things to do than hang out in the courtyard."

"Huh," Quincy said. "Seems like you didn't have anywhere better to be last Friday night."

"What are you talking about?" asked Addison. I stole a look at her. Her jaw was set in its usual fearless line. Heidi, on the other hand, was starting to look a bit ghostly.

"You know, when you were out here painting stupid pictures on the courtyard wall," Quincy said.

"Maybe you didn't notice because you were wearing earbuds and dancing to your own music like a freak," Addison hissed, "but we were at the dance. Just like you."

"You're right," Quincy agreed. "I had better things to do than watch where you were all night. But it doesn't matter what I noticed, because the security camera caught everything."

Addison laughed again. "That stupid camera caught *nothing*."

"Yeah," Heidi chimed in. "If that camera worked, why would Marcy be the one out here cleaning?"

Addison stepped on Heidi's toe. Hard. Now Heidi was the one with tears in her eyes.

"What do you mean, Heidi?" I asked. "Who *should* be the one out here cleaning?"

"Yeah," Quincy said quietly, stepping closer to them. "Is there any chance it was you guys? And maybe Amber? After the dance ended? It wouldn't have taken very long; I mean, this is terrible artwork."

"Whatever," said Addison. "So what if it was us. No one will ever know. Only losers get caught. And only even bigger losers like you guys would waste your time cleaning up after someone else."

Mr. Solo stepped out of his hiding spot behind the corner bushes. "So cleaning up after other people makes you a loser, huh?" he said. "Tell that to my kids who have a roof over their heads because of my job doing exactly that."

Now Addison was the one looking ghostly. (Heidi looked nearly comatose; I was waiting for her to pass out.)

"I wasn't—" Addison started to speak, but Mr. Solo cut her off.

"I think we've all heard just about enough out of you," he said. "It doesn't much matter now if that camera's broken, does it? We have a story to tell Principal Olin."

Addison was panicked. "There's no *story*. I'll say I was kidding. You're not even a teacher here. Why would she believe the *custodian* over one of her top students?"

Mr. Solo didn't respond. He didn't have to. The final visitor to the courtyard had arrived.

"Mr. Solo is one of the most trustworthy people I know, Addison," said Ms. Olin, stepping from the corridor into the courtyard doorway. "And I've been standing here long enough to know that you're quite the opposite, *top student* or not."

Possibly for the first time ever, Addison appeared to be speechless. And Heidi leaned against the wall, slid down to the ground, and burst into tears.

# 48. It's complicated

I got to my locker just before Davis Davis got to his this morning. I opened my lock in a blink and unzipped my backpack.

"Impressive!" said a voice behind me. It was Davis, of course.

"Ha," I said. "Practice makes perfect."

"You're even better at that than you are at graffiti," he said.

I squinted at him. "That wasn't me," I said. "I didn't do it."

He smiled. "I'm just messing with you," he said. "You might be annoying, but I know you aren't a criminal."

Some compliment. "How am I annoying?" I asked.

"You're the one who's always in my way, taking forever to open your lock!"

This time Davis squinted.

"I'm just messing with you!" I said, giving him a little smile as I closed my locker door.

He rolled his eyes. "Yeah, yeah," he said. "Happy Thanksgiving. Don't be a turkey."

A little joke! From Davis Davis! "Same to you, Davis," I said, and then I made a tiny gobbling sound before I walked away.

■ ■ ■

Like everyone else, Ms. Barakat had Thanksgiving on the brain the day before break. But unlike the other teachers who were showing movies or killing time by having us talk about our favorite Thanksgiving foods, Ms. Barakat was making us write.

"Thanksgiving is, for many people, a beautiful holiday," she said as we were taking our seats. "But it can also be a complicated holiday, can't it?"

She made a chart on the board, with THANKSGIVING across the top and two columns below that, one labeled BEAUTIFUL and the other labeled COMPLICATED.

"Let's think about this as a group first," she said. "Who has things we can put in each column?"

Eric's hand shot up. "Beautiful: mashed potatoes!" he said. "Ooh, and complicated: yams."

Ms. Barakat laughed. "Okay, I think those both are subject to debate, but we'll go with it for now." She wrote his suggestions on the board.

Mekhai raised his hand. "Beautiful: family." Ms. Barakat nodded and wrote *family* under *Beautiful*.

I thought for a second, then raised my hand when she turned back around. "Complicated: family."

A few kids laughed. Ms. Barakat smiled and nodded again, then wrote my suggestion on the board. No one argued with it, which I was grateful for as I felt my cheeks growing warm.

Eric raised his hand again. "Complicated: history."

Another nod from Ms. Barakat. "Can you say more about that?"

"The way the white settlers treated the native people. Not exactly something to be thankful for."

Marcy raised her hand. "Yeah. So I think 'feeling thankful' could also go on both sides."

"Okay, that's an interesting thought, Marcy," Ms. Barakat said, adding *feeling thankful* to both sides of the chart. "And you've also set me up nicely for today's assignment.

"Relax, it's not so bad," she said when a few kids groaned. "You may have to think a little, but I think you might enjoy it. I want you to do something you've probably been doing since kindergarten, and that's to tell me about what you're thankful for. But not just the basic, easy stuff, like your dog and your mashed potatoes. Although those things could certainly be included. Is there anything you're thankful for that's especially beautiful? Or even a bit more complicated? You can make a chart like this one, but you don't have to. And you don't even have to show this to me at the end of class. Just think and write for a while.

"Oh, and in case I forget to say it later, happy Thanksgiving."

I looked at the chart on the board. I looked out the window. I glanced at Addison and Heidi, who had definitely been quieter since the two-day suspension they got last week, for defacing school property and for failing to come forth as other students were punished for their crime. (Yeah, that was satisfying. I'm glad Mr. Solo and Ms. Olin were in the right place at the right time to catch those three in their lie. I guess there actually *can* be justice in middle school, Lou.)

I glanced at Marcy, who gave me a little smile as she fiddled with her butterfly earring. I looked at Ms. Barakat, who was twisting her hair into a lopsided bun as she read student papers.

I started writing.

*I am thankful that . . .*

1. *We get a four-day weekend, with no homework.*
2. *Mom and Dad are spending Thanksgiving together this year, and that I'm okay with it (unlike last year when Dad went to Uncle Keith's . . . although I was still okay with it, because for all of us to spend Thanksgiving together three weeks after they split up would have been way too awkward).*
3. *Ms. Olin believes us now.*
4. *My parents believed me almost from the beginning.*
5. *Ms. Olin also seems to have believed my anonymous note about the Gooser. Elaine told me she saw him going into her office the other day, and as far as*

I know, he hasn't pinched anyone since. (And I'll always be thankful to Elaine for tripping him at the dance!)

6. Mr. Solo says he'll help us make the courtyard as nice as it used to be, and we can even plant flower beds.

7. I have a happy, slobbery, goofy dog; even when I don't want humans in my personal space, I'm always okay snuggling with Iris. Dogs are different.

8. I have a job taking care of a cute little kid for a nice family who live on a secret road.

9. I'm going to meet Layla's guinea pig this weekend. She changed her name from Officer Nibbles to Muriel, which is fine with me. I've met enough officers this year.

10. I'm going to sleep over at Sarah's on Friday.

11. Uncle Keith is bringing his famous pumpkin cheesecake to Thanksgiving.

12. Mom's friend Bonnie is bringing her taco dip (even though it's not Thanksgiving-y, but she knows I love it).

13. *Mr. Singer. Well . . . I guess I'm thankful Mom has found someone nice, and that she seems really happy lately. But I'm also thankful that he's not coming to our Thanksgiving. Still too weird.*

14. *I have almost enough money saved for contacts. But I'm not in as much of a hurry to get them as I was a few months ago. I might even still wear my glasses once in a while after I buy them.*

15. *Even though I still wonder what people think of me (like, at least once a day), I don't worry about it as much. The people who I like, like me back. I know that's really all that matters.*

16. *I've gotten to know Syd, who will probably always eat tomatoes like they're apples, no matter what anyone says.*

17. *Elaine and Sarah became friends even without me making them do it.*

18. *I can talk to Sarah about Mom and Dad, and she never makes me feel weird.*

19. *Marcy seems like maybe she'll land somewhere between her old clingy self*

*and her newer Silver self, and maybe we*
*can be friends again?*

20. *Quincy saves me from losing my mind in*
    *homeroom and gym. And she makes me*
    *want to be brave.*
21. *Layla goes to a different middle school.*
    *Because now I know she'll always be*
    *my friend, but if she went to Meridian,*
    *I probably wouldn't have gotten to be*
    *friends with Sarah, and Elaine, and*
    *Quincy. And even Syd. And Nick.*
22. *Nick and I like the same music. And he*
    *makes me laugh. And even though I've*
    *known him since we were three, he still*
    *feels like a new friend somehow.*
23. *I might have found a village after all.*

The bell was about to ring. I opened my language-arts folder and was putting the thankful list in when I remembered something else.

24. *Also, I'm thankful for my little sister,*
    *Louie. Because she wrestles with Iris to*
    *distract her when Iris wants to eat my*
    *homework. And she actually is pretty*

*good at braiding hair, so I think I'll ask*
*her to braid mine on Thanksgiving. And*
*because she is trying to keep our special*
*family memories together in one little*
*shoebox. And because even though it*
*annoys me and I never really answer, it's*
*kind of sweet how she keeps asking me*
*what middle school is like.*

Here's the thing, Lou: middle school has felt so *big* to me. Not the building itself (although it is). But all of it: the classes, the homework, the teachers, the problems, the people. All the people.

Sometimes it feels so big that it takes up my whole life, and other things—like little sisters—get pushed into the corners. Does that make sense? Maybe not. But you'll see for yourself in a couple of years, Louie. And . . . you don't have to if you don't want to, but maybe then you can tell me about the people *you* meet in middle school.

# Acknowledgments

Many thanks to all the people I've met who helped this book come to life, starting with my incredibly talented critique partners, Ariel Bernstein, Ali Bovis, Katey Howes, and Emma Bland Smith (aka "the Pandas"). Their insights and encouragement were enormously helpful in shaping Gus and Louie's story.

I am grateful to my agent, Sarah Burnes, not only for her sage shepherding of my writing but also for her dedication to making the world a better place. Same for my friend, writing guide, and world-saving whiz Melissa Walker.

My editor, Julia Maguire, continues to amaze me with her knack for gently helping me discover exactly who my characters are and what they mean to each other. Working with her and the team at Knopf Books for Young Readers is a writer's dream come true. (This includes Artie Bennett, Marianne Cohen, Alison Kolani, and Karen Sherman, whose crackerjack copyediting skills bring to mind the work of masterful detectives!) And Hyesu Lee's art captures the whirl of middle-school life magnificently; I thank her for her wonderful rendering of Gus's world, and Bob Bianchini for his talent and dedication in perfecting the cover design.

This book would not exist without the stories shared by many friends who responded with truth, humor, and generosity to my email with the subject line "Tell me about your characters." I will not name names in the interests of privacy, but please know how very appreciative I am!

Howard McGinn and Mary Lou Keim McGinn deserve endless credit for giving me the courage to put words on paper over and over again, for decades. Jane and Samantha McGinn, thank you for your humor and heart.

Kevin McGinn, in addition to being an invaluable counselor, entertainer, and chef, is the one person who can take me back to childhood in a flash and (better still) make me laugh about it. I am also tremendously grateful for Emily Purchia's warm smile and spirited support.

My brilliant girls, Alice and Lucy Mahoney, you give

me hope and make me believe in good, even when the world is serving up the opposite. I think you're hilarious, I love to watch you sleep, and I secretly enjoy folding your laundry. (There, I said it.) Sadie Mahoney, you are a sweet furry mess. Thank you for keeping me on my feet. Literally.

Boundless gratitude to Whelan Mahoney, the kind, quirky, and steady soul of the whole operation.

Finally, to the people in all the villages I've been so lucky to find throughout my life: I thank you for making the journey interesting and joyful.